ROSE CAMPION
and the
CHRISTMAS MYSTERY

LYN GARDNER

First published in the UK in 2019 by Nosy Crow Ltd
The Crow's Nest, 14 Baden Place, Crosby Row
London, SE1 1YW, UK

www.nosycrow.com

ISBN: 978 1 78800 0314

Nosy Crow and associated logos are trademarks and/or
registered trademarks of Nosy Crow Ltd

A CIP catalogue record for this book will be available from the
British Library.

Printed and bound in the UK by Clays Ltd, Elcograf S.p.A.
Typeset by Tiger Media

Papers used by Nosy Crow are made from wood grown in
sustainable forests.

1 3 5 7 9 10 8 6 4 2

Prologue

The little door, set within the imposing wooden gates of Holloway prison, swung open, its hinges wheezing as if in complaint.

"'Ere you go, Duchess. Freedom. Enjoy it," said a ginger-whiskered prison warder, nodding his head towards the frozen city, still grey with sleep.

The woman stepped over the threshold and paused, huddled on the cobbles just a couple of steps beyond the small door. A ragged shawl covered her head. A few flecks of snow floated in the air. The warder eyed her curiously.

"Don't tell me you're reluctant to leave us, Duchess. What with everyone saying the only way you'd ever leave 'Olloway was in a box, I'd 'ave thought you'd scarper sharp, before thems who decide realise they made a mistake and banged you up again."

The woman didn't move. The warder's eyes narrowed. "Maybe it's true what they say. The Duchess is a broken woman, her power vanished. Just a shell picked clean by the scavengers." The warder spat towards the huddled figure and slammed the door shut with a smug smile, as if he was locking her out of Eden itself.

The woman waited a moment, and then raised her head and straightened her back. She let the ragged, spittle-covered shawl drop to the frosted ground and stood, ramrod straight, suddenly a tall imposing figure. She lifted her face to the thin rays of sun struggling to pierce a sky bloated with snow. The distant sound of hooves, flinty on cobbles, approached. The woman smiled, her eyes hard. A horse and carriage trotted into view. The carriage stopped and the driver bowed his head as if in respect. The carriage door opened and a man emerged, dapper in a frock coat and shoes that shone like polished sixpences.

"Duchess," he said with a low bow.

"You're late, Mr T," snapped the Duchess impatiently.

The man coughed nervously and nodded towards the interior of the carriage. "Someone has come to meet you, Duchess. I tried to prevent him, but…"

His voice quavered and trailed off, as if he feared her reaction. Like the imperious old Queen, Victoria, the Duchess – whose nickname reflected her status as criminal royalty, rather than any connections to the aristocracy – was not fond of surprises. She raised an eyebrow in question.

Mr T lowered his voice and whispered.

"The Cobra."

The Duchess's eyes brightened with interest. The Cobra was the nickname for Ambrose Skelly. Skelly had long been the king of London's criminal underworld. His nickname came about because those of his enemies who lived to tell the tale frequently said that an encounter with him felt like being mesmerised by a snake. It was a skill he had learned from his father, who, in the days before chloroform, had worked for a surgeon and was charged with calming the patients whose operations were conducted while they were still fully conscious.

The Cobra had been thought untouchable. But,

two months previously, his closest associates – including his own brother, eager to take over the Cobra's criminal empire for himself – had betrayed him to the police, providing the evidence that would ensure he was locked up for at least fifty years. The Cobra had evaded the police when they had tried to arrest him, and he had been on the run ever since. Although he was much younger than the Duchess, still only in his mid-thirties, they were old adversaries, with a genuine respect for each other.

The Duchess settled herself into the carriage with only a curt nod to the slender, handsome man with dark hair and delicate features, who sat well back on the opposite seat, clearly eager to avoid being spotted by anyone peering in. The Duchess stamped her foot twice and the carriage lurched forward across the rutted, icy road.

"What do you want, Ambrose?" asked the Duchess briskly.

"I want us to work together, Duchess," said the Cobra, smiling.

The Duchess's eyes glittered, her smile as thin as a snake's. "Don't you mean that you need my help, Ambrose? From what I hear you are a dead man walking. Hunted by the police and betrayed by your own flesh and bone. It can't be nice to be the hunted rather than the hunter. I could hand you in myself. I hear there is a handsome reward on your head."

Ambrose's eyes were wary but his smile was confident, showing a flash of surprisingly white teeth. "But you won't, will you, Duchess," he said leaning over and taking her hand and kissing it. He leaned further in and murmured. "For old time's sake."

The Duchess removed her hand. "Ambrose, you mistake me for a woman with a heart."

Ambrose put his head on one side, his eyes watchful.

"I know you are a practical woman, and we can be useful to each other. I need your brains and help to evade capture and to raise enough money to leave the country and start again. You are in need of ready cash to rebuild your empire. It has crumbled while you've been behind bars. You still have a few loyal acolytes like Mr T here, but I hear your intelligence network is destroyed. You are not the power you once were, Duchess."

"Well, that makes two of us, Ambrose," she replied tartly.

The Duchess settled back comfortably in the carriage and surveyed the street outside, her eyes greedy for the sights and sounds of London that she had been denied for so long. The city was waking up. Cafes were opening their doors, hoping to attract the sleepy-eyed seamstresses, porters and clerks who hurried past, shivering on their way to work. A muffin man was competing for custom with one of the coffee and bread-and-butter stalls. Hawkers were shouting their wares, offering everything from pots and pans to tiny birds in cages.

After a short silence, the Duchess continued. "If I were inclined to help you, what can you offer me?"

"Information. Useful information. Plenty of it. I still have connections in the higher reaches of society – more than one in the very heart of the aristocracy." The Duchess was silent again, patiently waiting for him to offer up a little nugget of information.

"The Easingford Emeralds. Edward Easingford will be bringing them to London very soon."

"Edward Easingford?" said the Duchess thoughtfully. "The one with connections to Campion's Palace of Variety and Wonders, where my double-dealing son met his end?"

Ambrose nodded. "Yes. The emeralds are worth a small fortune – enough to set us both up in our own ways. Several times over. If we could find a way to get our hands on them."

Ambrose smiled. He could see from the sparkle in her eyes that he had piqued the Duchess's interest.

A small boy, selling newspapers, was shouting over the din as the carriage moved through the narrow streets, into the heart of the city. The carriage rolled past the Alhambra and ground to a halt outside the Empire Theatre of Varieties in Leicester Square. It was immediately surrounded by chestnut sellers and hawkers with trays of sheep trotters and hot green peas. The Duchess batted them away with her hand, as if dismissing tiresome flies.

Outside the Alhambra a man was pasting that coming night's bill on to the wall – a list promising marvels and wonders, including George the Talking Pig, the Flying Fongoli Brothers, and Luella, "the beautiful girl acrobat and human cannonball". The Duchess suddenly sat up a little straighter. Her gaze was directed towards another poster on the music-hall wall, informing the public of the arrival later that week of Madame Elenora de Valentina. "Direct from New York! The famed hypnotist and Wonder of the Age! Her mind rules the world!"

The Duchess was silent for so long that Ambrose wondered whether she had fallen asleep, when suddenly she spoke.

"Mr T, put your head in the stage door and enquire when Miss de Valentina is expected to be arriving and where. Oh, and find out if she was booked unseen or if anyone from the hall has actually met her. Use a little bribery if you must."

Mr T left the coach. The Duchess appeared to be engrossed in watching the elephants, who were being given their breakfast outside the theatre. More flakes of snow began to fall, dancing like moths around the animals' huge ears.

Presently, Mr T returned. "She arrives on Wednesday at Euston on the boat train. The act was booked unseen."

The Duchess smiled. "Perfect. We will arrange a welcoming party for little Nell Valentine – or whatever she's calling herself these days."

"Do you know her, Duchess?" asked Ambrose.

"I may be mistaken, but I believe I do. But it is of no consequence, whether it is the same woman or not. She serves my purpose now." She smiled at the Cobra.

"I think we can do business, Ambrose. I have a plan."

He leaned forward eagerly to hear.

The Duchess's eyes turned dark and she hissed in his face. "We will work together, and you will follow my instructions. But I warn you, Ambrose – if you try to double-cross me, I will have your guts for garters."

1

Rose Campion gave another bow to the cheering audience, up on its feet and roaring its delight. Then she ran off stage and skidded straight into a large wooden box. It was cramped backstage at Campion's Palace of Varieties and Wonders, the music hall where Rose had been found abandoned as a baby by Thomas Campion. Thomas had given Rose his name and a home. The box was taking up more than its fair share of the space available.

"Ouch!" squeaked Rose crossly, as she hopped on one leg holding her shin, and then she turned, a wide smile pasted across her face despite the pain, and ran back on stage into the bright lights to acknowledge the cheers of the crowd. The show had to go on, even if Rose could feel the blood trickling down her leg. She curtseyed deeply and then exited again, as the music swelled and the ballet girls ran on from the other side of the stage and began an exuberant high-kicking routine.

"Here," said Effie, handing Rose a not entirely pristine handkerchief, which she appeared to have been using to grease the backstage pulleys. "That should stem the worst of the bleeding." Effie grinned. "It went well, Rosie. They lapped it up. Them limericks you've written are something different. Very witty. We should use some of them in the pantomime, if Thomas ever makes up his mind what title we're going to do this year. But for now, I reckon you've got a real hit on your hands. Thomas'll be ever so proud when he sees it. You should have let him come tonight."

"I just wanted to do it for the first time without him there, in case I made an idiot of myself. Besides, he needed to go and visit Pru and her poor sick mum," said Rose, perching on the edge of the box and dabbing at the gash in her leg. She looked thoughtful. "I enjoyed it, but it's not nearly as fun as doing the bicycle turn with Rory. We were so close to having a completely new act ready, and then she suddenly abandoned it and swanned off to Silver Square with Edward to play at being lords and ladies. I don't understand the two of them. I thought they were done with all that being-a-toff stuff."

The fact that Aurora – or Rory, as she was known by her friends – was the daughter of a lord, and sometimes mixed in aristocratic circles, was a source of tension between her and Rose, who couldn't understand why anyone would want to waste time in Mayfair drawing rooms when they could spend every minute in the warm, welcoming, riotous fug of Campion's. Aurora and her father Edward – an actor who had unexpectedly discovered that he was the rightful heir to a title, a London house and a country estate – said that they wanted nothing more than to be permanently based at Campion's. But they kept being drawn back into the orbit of London's high society. Aurora and Edward were still getting to know each other, having been parted since Rory was a tiny baby, and sometimes Rose thought it was like watching two well-meaning strangers trying to dance together and tripping over each other's feet.

"They'll be back soon enough, Rosie," said Effie soothingly. "Rory and Eddie will return in plenty of time for rehearsals for the panto. They're only staying at Silver Square because Grace has come to London to buy her trousseau for her wedding to that Sir Godfrey Caskins. If she's marrying a gentleman she can hardly stay here at Campion's. Toffs like him wouldn't think it was proper. They say he's got pots of money. There was a big article in *The Times* about him. Apparently he does good everywhere he goes. I've met plenty of them do-gooders, and they're always very la-di-dah."

Rose was certain that Grace, a former aerial contortionist and widow of Edward's cousin, would have much preferred to spend her time at Campion's, rather than playing cards in Silver Square with elderly aristocrats, but Edward had insisted that Grace would want a glimpse into London society after months of being alone in Yorkshire, with only her little son Freddie for company.

Edward had expressed his concern to Rory that Grace might not be marrying Sir Godfrey because she really loved him, but because she was lonely and wanted for company. But Rory had told Rose and Effie that she thought that was unlikely, because while Godfrey Caskins may be saintly, he was also one of the most boring men she had ever met.

Rose sighed. "I do so miss Rory."

"Well," said Effie good-humouredly, "until Rory returns, you'll just have to make do with me."

Rose grinned. It was never a hardship spending time with Effie. An orphan who at one time had been set to work as a pickpocket against her will, Effie was as much like a sister to Rose as Aurora. It felt odd being two when they were normally three. Rose thought it was like having a limb missing.

"Come on, Effie, we better shift this box. If we leave it here there'll be a bloodbath when the ballet girls all try and exit the stage." She looked at the mysterious box with curiosity. "What's in it, anyway? And who does it belong to?"

"I don't know what's in it, but I know it's for that Desiree, or whatever she calls herself," said O'Leary, who happened to be passing. The elderly actor was employed as the Campion's stage-door keeper – a job that his fondness for brandy made him quite ill-suited to carry out with any efficiency. But he was as much a part of Campion's as the gilt mirrors and gas lamps.

The way he sniffed made it clear what he thought about Desiree, the star dancer who had been packing out Campion's for weeks with her dance of the seven veils. Desiree – real name Ivy Puddlewick – was as popular with the Campion's punters as she was unpopular with the Campion's staff and other performers.

When she had first arrived at Campion's, everyone had felt sorry for Ivy, who, like far too many ballet girls in music halls and theatres across the land, had had the misfortune to be badly burned while performing. Her costume had caught alight on the gas lamps while dancing at a hall on the Walworth Road. Ivy had been one of the lucky ones – she didn't die, but her neck and chin were badly scarred. She had turned terrible adversity to her advantage, coming up with a new act in which she billed herself as "the greatest sensation since Salome" and performed a dance in which the lower half of her face remained covered even after she had removed her other veils. It was a wily trick that highlighted the soulful expressiveness of her sad, dark eyes, which she liberally outlined with burned cork. But success had gone to Ivy's head. She had turned into something of a monster – refusing to share a dressing room and treating everyone at Campion's as if they were the dirt on the underside of her boots.

Thomas, who hated such behaviour, had been on the verge of not renewing Ivy's weekly contract, when his other star turn, Prudence Smith, whose stage name was the far more alluring Belle Canterbury, had taken time off again to nurse her invalid mother, Giovanna. Mrs Smith, a tiny bird-like woman, Italian by birth, had been at death's door for at least ten years, but so far had always remained on the right side of it. Pru joked that her ma would outlive them all.

With Belle Canterbury – her major competition – absent, Desiree became more popular than ever. Every night a queue of young men gathered around the Campion's stage door, clutching bouquets and hoping for a private audience with Desiree. Their hopes were almost always dashed. Ivy was smart enough to realise that the success of her act was enhanced by cultivating an air of mystery. Rose had noticed that lately Ivy had taken to wearing a pair of diamond earrings, which rather suggested she had an affluent admirer – but if she did, she was keeping him a secret.

Approaches from Dottie Collins – billed as "the Queen of the Swells", who did a very successful comic song and dance routine – and Hopkin and Dent, a pair of illusionists who took it in turns to stroll around the stage with the other's disembodied head under their arms, had failed to dislodge Ivy from the top of the Campion's bill.

"I suspect the only thing that will do it is death," said Lottie, the lead ballet girl, one afternoon, after Ivy had been particularly vile. "But she can't be more than twenty-two, so we may have a very long wait," she added gloomily.

Rose peered through one of several small holes punched into the side of the mysterious box. But the interior was far too dark for her to see anything. The music from the orchestra indicated that the dance routine was reaching its climax.

"Come on, Effie. It's now or never if we're going to move this box. We can haul it into Ivy's dressing room, and then it's her problem, not ours." Rose and Effie each took a side of the box and lifted it a few inches off the ground. Immediately there was a strange noise from within. The girls dropped the box in surprise.

"It's alive!" shrieked Effie. "It's a snake!"

Rose shook her head. "Snakes definitely don't growl." She fixed an eye to one of the holes and looked down into the box. Two yellow eyes glared back at her.

"It's a cat," said Rose excitedly. "Somebody has given Ivy a cat."

"Poor puss," said Effie with sympathy. "I don't think being owned by Ivy would be much fun. I saw her aim a kick at Ophelia the other day." Ophelia was the Campion's cat, who treated the music hall as if it was her own personal fiefdom. At this very moment she was curled up at the far side of the stage, watching the ballet girls dance, and purring contentedly.

"Let's free it," said Rose. "I bet it can hardly breathe with these tiny air holes. I don't care if Ivy screams blue murder. It's cruel to keep it confined any longer. If Ivy doesn't want it, it can stay here at Campion's."

Rose had found a claw hammer and was already removing the nails in the top of the box. The growling was getting louder.

"This little puss has got a splendid pair of lungs," said Rose as she started to pull the lid up.

"I don't know why they put it in such a big—" Effie didn't finish the sentence, because at that moment the lid came away and there was a streak of black stripes on reddish fur, as the animal jumped out of the box, caught sight of Ophelia on the other side of the stage and gave what sounded like a delighted purr.

"That's not a cat, that's a tiger cub!" said Rose, as the tiger launched itself across the stage, scattering the startled ballet girls like skittles in an arcade. Ophelia took one look at this giant cat, gave a mew of surprise and leapt off the stage and into the auditorium, with the excited tiger cub in hot pursuit. A roar of elation tinged with fear went up from the audience as the two cats streaked through the theatre, tripping up one of the bar staff carrying a tray loaded with full glasses and plates of sprats and beef and kidney pies, and tore back towards the stage, leaving chairs and tables overturned in their wake as the crowd jostled for room and tried to stay out of their path.

The animals circled around the stage again,

while Rose tried to grab the tiger cub, but its beautiful soft fur slipped through her fingers. She shouted to Effie and the ballet girls to block the tiger's path, but nobody was prepared to stand firm when faced with the surprisingly solid bulk of the cub hurtling towards them.

Still hotly pursued, Ophelia shot off the stage and out of the stage door, leaping on to the roof of the workshop. She would have jumped the gate if Thomas, on his way in, had not flung it wide open. For a moment he looked astonished as both Ophelia and the tiger cub flew by him, followed by Rose and Effie. The girls came to a halt and watched as the two cats raced down Hangman's Alley, causing a horse to rear and upsetting a cart full of potatoes in the lane beyond, before streaking away in the direction of the Thames.

Thomas picked up his hat and raised an eyebrow at Rose.

"Another quiet, uneventful night in my absence then," he said quizzically. "But you know I don't really hold with wild-animal acts, Rose." Rose could see that Thomas's eyes were crinkled and he looked tickled. She hoped that when he saw the devastation inside he would still be amused.

"Me neither," said Rose. "This one made an unscheduled appearance on the bill. It was in a box delivered to Ivy. A present, I imagine, from one of her more foolish admirers."

"Ah," said Thomas, as if that explained everything. One of the things Rose loved about Thomas was his ability to remain unruffled, even when complete chaos had broken out around him. "I do hope that Ophelia will be all right."

"I think the tiger cub just wanted to play," said Rose. It had begun to snow again, the flakes hitting the frosty yard, which shimmered in the moonlight. Rose shivered. "Ophelia has still got at least seven of her nine lives. I'm more worried about the cub. Will it survive outside in this weather?"

Thomas nodded.

"If I'm not mistaken, I believe it was a Siberian tiger. They don't mind the cold. Although it may give some of Southwark's residents a bit of a fright. I'll contact the Zoological Gardens first thing in the morning – I'm sure they'll be able to find and house it. A tiger cub roaming the streets can do little harm, but in a month or so when it's bigger it could be a different matter."

They went inside, and, to Rose's relief, the damage amounted to little more than a few upturned tables and chairs. The entertainment was already back in full swing – Dolores was doing her hair-hanging act, in which she suspended herself from the roof with a wire that passed through her top-knot.

Rose, Effie and Thomas stood together at the side of the stage, watching and trying not to wince. They all knew that hair-hanging hurt like mad.

"How were Pru and Mrs Smith?" asked Effie.

"Mrs Smith is much better – Pru thinks her mother is going to pull through again. With any luck we might have Belle Canterbury back on the bill next week. If we settle on *Cinderella* for the pantomime, she can play Prince Charming."

"Maybe Ivy can play the wicked stepmother. She wouldn't have to act much," joked Rose, and blushed when she saw Thomas frown, although he couldn't quite disguise the twinkle in his eye.

"How did the new act go, Rosie?"

"Brilliantly," said Effie, seeing Rose's hesitation. "It's a proper cracker. The crowd loved it."

"Does that mean that you'll let me watch it tomorrow night?" asked Thomas. Rose nodded shyly.

"Good," said Thomas with a smile. "It's a bit rum when I'm not allowed to watch an act in my own music hall performed by my own daughter." Rose gave him a covert look. It was rare for Thomas to ever lay claim to her as his daughter. Once she would have resented it, but not now. Thomas had always been completely honest with her about her origins – abandoned on the steps of Campion's as a tiny baby. She was almost thirteen – perhaps it was time to acknowledge that after all these years she was never going to find her real parents. Rory may have found her long-lost father, but that was a miracle. It wasn't going to happen twice.

2

It was late morning and Rose and Effie were on their way to Euston Station to collect a parcel for Thomas that was arriving on the boat train from Liverpool.

They had spent the early morning searching for the tiger cub. Ophelia had turned up back at Campion's at dawn, waking Rose by jumping on to the bed and digging her claws into the bedclothes. It was rare for the cat to be absent all night, and she had a look on her face of deep satisfaction.

Rose had roused Effie and they had set out on their search at first light. The freezing fog slid in from the river like a cold, clammy hand clawing at their faces. In a narrow alleyway behind St Olave's churchyard, where Effie's poor mother, who had died in Holloway prison, was buried, they had found two sets of cat prints – one big and one small – on an otherwise unmarked carpet of snow. They met people whose stories made them suspect the cub must be close by. A milk woman, her pails swinging from a wooden yoke over her shoulders, expressed anger at finding knocked-over pails of milk in the cow stall and telltale feline footprints. A butcher, who had been at work since three a.m., told them of "the monster cat" snaffling meat from his shop when he had briefly left the back door open. Down by the river the ragged mudlarks were full of the wondrous sight they had witnessed: a tiger and a tabby cat sitting together on the Devil's Steps in Bermondsey, licking each other's fur. But the girls didn't catch the tiniest glimpse of the tiger cub. On their return to Campion's they had told Thomas of their discoveries. He had contacted the Zoological Gardens' director, Mr Burns, who was getting together a search party with a net.

"The cub won't be able to hide undetected for too long in this part of the city," said Thomas. "There are far too many people for it to go unspotted. I just hope the zoo gets to it before anyone more unscrupulous. That beautiful fur would be worth a bob or two. Or a travelling circus would be keen to find it if they get wind that it's on the loose."

Rose hoped that the Zoological Gardens found the tiger cub before anyone else hunted it down in the narrow streets of Bermondsey. It would be sad to see the animal behind bars in the zoo, but exploitation or death would be worse – and the Tanner Street boys would be after the animal if they realised they could make some money from its skin.

She and Effie arrived at the station just a few minutes after the boat train had arrived. Porters were scurrying around as trunks and carpetbags were unloaded. Rose thought it exciting to watch people walk down the platform – people who, just ten days before, would have been standing on a different continent. She gazed around at the crowds waiting by the barrier, a mixture of family members and servants and hansom cab drivers, some holding signs proclaiming the names of the people they had come to meet, others simply scanning faces.

She and Effie nodded at a man with a shock of red hair, who they recognised as Pony Snatchwitch, one of the stagehands from the

Alhambra Music Hall in Leicester Square. He was standing a little way away from the crowds gathered around the platform entrance, and he had a small sign on which was scrawled the name "Miss Elenora de Valentina" in spidery writing. But he wasn't holding it aloft like others waiting for passengers – he was too busy smoking and talking animatedly to a young woman who, to his evident delight, was flirting with him.

A child ran down the platform into the arms of her mother, and for a moment Rose wondered what it would feel like to be running into her own mother's arms. At the far end of the platform she could see a woman walking towards the concourse – a lithe, elegant, dark-haired figure dressed in a blue suit, whose head was dipped in a way that made Rose think of a shy swan. She was carrying a small leather portmanteau. She was too far away for Rose and Effie to make out her features clearly, but for a moment Rose imagined what it would be like if this woman was her mother, and the two of them were about to discover each other for the first time and fall into each other's arms.

Her daydream was broken by Effie tugging at her sleeve. One of the porters from the parcel office indicated that he wanted the girls to accompany him. Rose and Effie followed the porter, and as they got to the office Rose glanced back across the station, just in time to see the woman in the blue suit being greeted by a woman in a large hat with a veil, and two men.

In the parcel office there were forms to be filled in in triplicate, and then the parcel had been mislaid. Almost thirty minutes had elapsed by the time Rose and Effie emerged, clutching the package containing the small piece of machinery that Thomas had ordered. By the time they were back on the station concourse, some luggage was still being unloaded from the boat train, but the passengers had all dispersed.

Only Pony Snatchwitch from the Alhambra was still standing by the platform entrance with his sign, looking uncertain.

Effie smiled at him and said, "What happened to your lady friend, Pony?"

He looked cross. "She was all over me like a rash, and then just as suddenly she lost interest and walked off!"

"Didn't Miss Elenora de Valentina turn up?"

The man scratched his head. "Must have missed her. Teach me to pay attention. Maybe she thought nobody was here to meet her and got herself a cab. No point hanging around here. Her luggage will be sent on to the Alhambra. I better go back and check she's there. I'm going to be in the doghouse if I've lost the Alhambra's latest star turn."

"What's her act?" asked Effie curiously.

"Some kind of silly hypnotism and mind-reading business," said Snatchwitch a little grumpily. "Apparently her mind rules the world."

"Oh well then," said Rose with a grin. "No need for you to worry. If her mind rules the world she should have no difficulty making it across London to Leicester Square on her own."

With much laughter, Rose and Effie were regaling Aurora with what had happened at Campion's the week before with the tiger cub.

"Oh, how I wish I'd been there," said Rory, and there was such wistfulness in her voice that Rose stopped herself from saying that Rory could have been if she hadn't run off to Silver Square. She knew she would regret such words as soon as they were out of her mouth. It wasn't Aurora's fault that she was so torn between her old life in the music hall and her new life as a lady.

Word had got around about what had happened with the tiger at Campion's, and the place had been packed ever since. Any out-of-the-ordinary happening or notoriety was always good for business. After a famous diamond, known as the Doomstone, had been stolen during a performance at Campion's, the hall had been packed for weeks afterwards.

Rose had already done her new act of witty ditties and limericks on the early bill of the night, and Thomas continued to be as delighted by its novelty as the Campion's crowd.

"You're a clever girl, Rose Campion," he said, and Rory, who had come over from Silver Square especially to see it, despite the fact that snow was falling heavily, was in agreement.

"It'll be such a hit you won't ever want to do the new bicycle act with me," she said.

"I'll always want to do the new bicycle act with you, Rory," said Rose quietly, and she saw the pleasure and relief in Rory's features.

"Oh I don't know," said Rory lightly. "You'll be knocking Desiree off the top of the bill soon, won't she, Thomas?"

Thomas laughed. "There are certainly plenty trying. Yesterday those illusionists, Hopkin and Dent, made another enquiry about top billing, and I had an approach this morning from a woman called Madame de Valentina.

Apparently, she's doing a roaring trade at the Alhambra."

Rose and Effie starred at each other. It was an odd coincidence. Thomas noticed their looks.

"Have you come across her? I thought she was fresh from New York."

"We just happened to be at Euston when she was supposed to be arriving on the boat train. But Pony Snatchwitch was otherwise engaged and missed her. Clearly Miss Valentina found her way to the Alhambra. Strange she wants to move on so quickly if she's doing so well there."

"She's a genuine hit," said Thomas. "I checked with the gaffer, Sam Collins. He was narked she was looking to move to Campion's. Of course, she may just be testing her worth and looking to get Sam to raise her wages. It's of no concern to me – as long as Ivy is top of the bill, there's no spot for Madame de Valentina here. She does seem very keen to perform here though, although I can't see why. There's more money in it for her at the Alhambra – it's so much bigger."

"That's true, but it's not as classy. The toffs and all their servants don't go there so often, and everyone knows that Campion's means quality," said Rory proudly. "It's good for any act to be associated with that. Anyway, how is our dear Ivy?"

"Dreadful!" said Rose and Thomas so completely in unison that they both burst out laughing.

"She's taking the disappearance of her tiger cub badly," said Rose. "Blames me and Effie and is demanding Thomas compensate her for her loss, even though Lottie and the other ballet girls says she hates cats because they make her eyes stream. Oh, and she was foul to Dolores, and she lost her temper with the stagehands again this afternoon. I heard several of them say they could happily kill her. She is such a cow you could boil her down and turn her into beef tea."

"Rose!" said Aurora in shocked tones.

"You can't deny it. Campion's would be a happier place without her."

"I know I should terminate her contract," said Thomas ruefully. "But for all her unpleasantness, I can't help wanting to give her as long as I can. When she's in a good mood she has a nice wry sense of humour. I suspect she hasn't had an easy life, and undoubtedly she will know hardship again. The crowd will eventually tire of her – her moment will be over, and then what will she do? I hear there are already copycat Salome acts all over town. Let her enjoy her little patch of sunlight before she ceases to be a crowd-puller and slips further and further down the bill."

"Do we know who sent her the tiger cub?" asked Aurora.

"Ivy wouldn't say when Lottie asked her," said Effie, who had just joined them, her hands covered in grease after spending hours mending the flying rig.

"But I saw the label. Ivy must have thrown it away in the kitchen rubbish. It said," Rose put on an exaggerated posh voice, "'A little tiger for my own little tiger from her favourite tiger hunter.'"

Aurora snorted with derision.

"The rubbish was the right place for it," said Thomas. He shook his head ruefully. "I fear the future might not be nearly as bright for Ivy as she likes to think it is – or, at least, pretends it is. She is all bluff and bluster."

Rose suddenly felt chastened. Few of those working in the music halls had the kind of security that she had at Campion's – a place she was lucky enough to call home. There would always be a spot for her here, even if she couldn't work. She resolved to bite her tongue and try and be nicer to Ivy in the future.

"Thomas," she asked, "are you quite settled on *Cinderella* for the Campion's pantomime this year?"

Thomas nodded. "We'll start rehearsals the Monday after next. Ivy will play Cinders, Pru will be back and can play Prince Charming, I want you, Effie, to do your magic act, which we'll work in as the centrepiece entertainment at the ball, and," he turned to Rose and Aurora, "I wondered whether you two might have fun playing the Ugly Sisters. We'll have them doing a comedy turn on the bicycle at one point."

"I'd love that," said Rose, delight making her eyes dance and sparkle, before she caught sight of Aurora's face.

Rory was biting her lip, and couldn't – or wouldn't – meet Rose's eye. "I'd have loved that too, but I can't, Thomas – not this year, not with the wedding and everything. I'm going to be a bridesmaid. It wouldn't be fair on Grace if I was parading all over Campion's stage just as she's getting married. People would talk. I hope you understand, Thomas."

"Of course," he said a little too heartily. "We all understand." He gave Rose a searching look, but she was too busy trying not to let the lump in her throat turn to tears to notice. Rose wanted to be generous towards Aurora, but she felt as if her friend was drifting further and further away from her, until a point would come when she was entirely out of reach.

"Excuse me," she said rather stiffly. "I'd better go and collect some glasses and plates for the bar. Before they're overwhelmed. If business keeps on as good as this, Thomas, we're going to need some extra help in the kitchen. They're barely coping." She walked away, and had just picked up a pile of plates when Lottie grabbed her by the arm.

"A couple of them mudlark children are at the door. Says they got summut you might be interested in."

Rose took a couple of hot mutton pies from the kitchen and walked briskly to the stage door. Two undersized children were waiting for her there, clutching a soaked leather portmanteau. She took the holdall from them and stuffed the pies into their hands, and the children couldn't put them in their mouths fast enough. She wondered how long it was since they had last eaten properly.

"How are you, Jess, Ossy?"

"We're fine, Rosie. But me dad's really worried," said Jess, a string bean of a ten-year-old. "This woman, a lady, she was hanging around asking him all sorts of questions. Says our dad's name is on some list in St Olave's for receiving charity. But he ain't had a farthing. He applied for alms, but the committee turned 'im down. Always do. They're as mean as dust. They sit there in their smart clothes and say they can't 'elp us cos we don't 'elp ourselves. As if being born poor is our fault."

"Well, if this woman gives you any trouble, come and see us, and Thomas will sort it out," said Rose. She looked at the portmanteau. The mudlark children often brought her items that they had dredged from the Thames or that had been washed up on the riverbank. She had come by the bicycle that she and Rory used in their double act that way, and she was always willing to part with a few shillings for things that might be useful to use as props.

The portmanteau was empty and ruined by

its soaking, and Campion's had plenty of such items in the prop cupboard, but she couldn't bear to dash the gleam of hope in the children's eyes. Someone at Campion's would find some use for it, even if just for storage, once it had dried out.

"Have you showed it to the police? It may help them identify someone if a body has been pulled out of the Thames," said Rose to the two children. Bodies were regularly found in the river, some with their throats cut or gashes to the head. The taller of the two children nodded.

"Only one poor soul pulled out of the Thames in the last few days. Murdered. A woman. Throat slashed. The police said they didn't think it belonged to her."

"All right. Wait a minute," said Rose, still clutching the portmanteau, and she went to the bar, got three shillings out of the till and gave them to the children, who whooped with joy and ran off into the night, their shoeless feet and ragged clothes no defence against the falling snow. Rose took the portmanteau to the props cupboard. As she put it down her hand grazed the clasp and she realised something was engraved there. She looked at the letters:

NV. She wondered what they stood for, and how the portmanteau had ended up in the river. She guessed it was probably stolen, the contents emptied out and the case then slung in the water. She just hoped that it was only the portmanteau, and not its owner, who had ended up in the Thames.

Rose could hear Thomas at the end of the corridor, asking if anyone had seen her. She knew he was checking that she was not upset by Aurora's reluctance to appear in the pantomime. She stepped out of the props room with a bright smile pasted across her face, ready to greet him, and she promptly forgot all about the portmanteau.

4

Two days later Aurora was back at Campion's with her father, Edward, and a group that, besides Grace and her fiancé, Sir Godfrey Caskins, also included several members of the aristocracy. In their fancy clothes the party immediately attracted the good-natured ribbing of the Campion's crowd. Grace was delighted to see Rose and Thomas and hugged them effusively.

"It's so lovely to be back at Campion's," she said. "I'd forgotten how full of life it is, and how alive it makes you feel. I have missed it." She looked wistful.

"We've missed you. You know you're welcome any time, Grace," said Thomas. "There would always be a place on the bill for you."

Grace blushed. "I'm very tempted, but I'm not sure my future husband would be amused," she said lightly. Rose was opening her mouth to say that a husband who didn't approve of a wife with a music-hall act might not be the right husband for Grace when she saw Thomas's warning look. Grace lowered her voice and said quickly, "Sir Godfrey is not entirely comfortable with my origins in the music hall. Of course, he knows – how could he not? He will have heard the gossip and the rumours, but he acts as if he has never heard a whisper about me. As far as he is concerned I'm the widow of Edward's cousin and therefore a lady."

"Then we will all be the souls of discretion," said Thomas a little too heartily. "Even Rose." He winked. "Although discretion goes against Rose's nature." He smiled at Grace. "Are you going to introduce us to your fiancé?"

Grace called to a well-dressed man who was talking animatedly to Edward. He turned and beamed at Thomas, bowed and held out his hand. Catching a glimpse of his ruddy face, Rose felt quite certain she had seen him at Campion's before on several occasions. But what he said suggested otherwise.

"Mr Campion," said Sir Godfrey. "I'm delighted to visit the legendary Campion's music hall at last. Edward has told me all about its charms. I'm glad to get the chance to see it for myself."

He waved an arm around vaguely as if trying to think how to describe it. "It's very quaint."

Rose caught Rory's eye, and both girls tried not to laugh. If there was anything that Thomas detested, it was hearing Campion's called "quaint" by patronising members of the aristocracy. The group took their seats, their silk dresses and glossy black tailcoats a stark contrast with the rest of audience, many of whom were decidedly shabby, if not downright ragged. Champagne arrived, and plates piled high with food.

On stage Dolores was doing her slack wire act, and Sir Godfrey was clapping as enthusiastically as anyone. Rose saw Grace watching him, and thought she detected a fleeting look of sadness in her eyes.

"Rory," she whispered. "Do you think Grace is genuinely happy about marrying Sir Godfrey?"

Aurora shrugged.

"I suppose she must be. Otherwise why

would she be marrying him? There's no reason except love. Edward has made it perfectly clear that Grace is welcome to stay at Easingford Hall as long as she wants. After all, Grace's son is his heir just as long as he has no son of his own. But it's more than that – Edward really likes Grace. They get on so well together. In fact, I always wondered whether they might marry one day. But clearly that's not to be. She has decided on Sir Godfrey. But as a measure of his esteem, Edward is going to give her the Easingford Emeralds as a wedding gift."

"Of course he is," said Rose with a wicked smile. "Just like Thomas and I are going to give Grace the Campion's tin plate tiara if we can bear to part with it. What exactly are the Easingford Emeralds when they're at home?"

Aurora blushed and continued quite huffily.

"They're quite famous actually. It's a necklace. Very simple but rather beautiful. I tried it on. I must say I rather liked how they looked, but Grace has always admired them too. They are worth a small fortune, but I don't think Grace realises that, which is just as well, or she would never accept the gift."

"That's incredibly generous of Edward,"

said Rose. "Wouldn't he want to keep them in the family? Maybe for you one day?" Aurora blushed.

"Well, they are very lovely. But Edward explained that he wants Grace to be going into the marriage with her own financial security. He has brought the emeralds with him – they're currently safe in the bank. He's going to present them to Grace at a dinner in her honour at Silver Square a couple of days before the wedding."

"A dinner? Will we be invited?" asked Rose, a little too sharply. There was a tiny beat, and Aurora's eyes filled with tears. "We're not snobs, Rose. Thomas is Edward's most trusted friend. Grace adores you all. Of course you'll be invited."

Yet again Rose felt guilty. Why couldn't she keep her tongue under control?

"Oh, Rory, I didn't mean to needle you. It's just – you must realise that there's a world of difference between toffs like Sir Godfrey and his friends coming to Campion's, and Campion's invading the drawing room of Silver Square."

"Of course I understand that, Rose. All too well. But if they don't like it, they will have to be the ones to stay away. The people we want there are our real friends. The ones who will stick by us through thick and thin. Edward and my connection with Campion's is no secret."

Rose frowned. "It's odd though, isn't it, that all those lords and ladies are just fine about Edward acting in plays in the West End, or appearing on the stage here at Campion's, but poor Grace doesn't want to publicly acknowledge she was once a music-hall performer. It's as if there is one rule for him, and quite another for her."

Aurora smiled sadly. "It's because we are women. It's all right for a lord to appear on the music-hall stage if he chooses – in fact, it's seen as delightfully eccentric. But my doing the same is viewed as scandalous. I'll never understand all these unwritten rules these fancy people seem to have." She put her arm through Rose's. "At least with you and Effie I know you'll always be on my side, whatever I do."

Rose grinned, delighted to have made her peace with her friend.

"Who's that?" she asked, nodding towards a woman seated at the table with Edward's party, who was leaning towards Grace and Edward and speaking quietly. She was more austerely dressed than Grace, and her hair was cut daringly short, chestnut curls coiled around the nape of her neck. Her laughing eyes, crinkled at the corners, lent her face an animated beauty. Edward and Grace's laughter rose at something she had said. There was something about the woman that attracted Rose to her. As if she knew her – although Rose was quite certain that she had never seen her before.

"Oh, that's Perdita Black," said Aurora. "She was raised in India by an uncle who organised big-game hunts. After he was mauled to death by a tiger, she was sent back to England to train to be a governess. But then she ran away to become an actress. And then for some reason she gave it up and became a governess after all. She was Freddie's governess for a few months, before he was sent away to school. She only mentioned her theatrical connections once she had the job, after she realised that Edward was an actor too, and that Grace had performed in a music hall. She stayed on as a companion for Grace when Freddie went away to school. I'll introduce you later. You'll like her. I do. She came from Lady Squawker with glowing references."

"Ah, the Squawkers," said Rose with a poker face. "I know the Bermondsey branch of the family well. Pie men down Marsh Street." She was pleased to see Aurora grin.

"Actually," said Rory, "the Mayfair Squawkers had terrible luck not long after after Perdita left them. They lost all the family heirlooms in a robbery."

"Shame," said Rose thinking of the mudlark children. "It must have been tough to be down to their last five bob."

Rory grinned. "Actually, I think it was their last £10,000."

* ✳ *

The ballet girls were doing their daisy flower routine on stage, whirling in yellow and white costumes, and Rose could feel the expectation rising in the auditorium in anticipation of Ivy's imminent appearance.

Rose left her seat and slipped backstage to find Effie, who was helping out on costumes. Ivy was standing at the side of the stage while Effie painstakingly secured her veils in place. It was a tricky job: if they were not attached sufficiently well, the veils fell prematurely, and if they were pinned too tightly, Ivy couldn't get them off at the crucial moment. Rose took some pins and started to help Effie.

"Watch out!" shrieked Ivy. "Are you trying to kill me, jabbing me in the head like that?"

"Sorry," said Rose meekly. "I'll be as gentle as I can." She secured another veil. "Ivy," she said, "do you ever think about the future? What you'll do when your Salome act stops being so popular?" She saw Ivy's big eyes blinking at her suspiciously from behind the gauzy layers.

"What you getting at, Rose Campion? Are you saying Thomas is going to let me go?"

"No, I didn't mean that at all. Thomas was only saying the other day that he thought you'd be top of the bill for ages yet." Ivy's shoulders relaxed, which endeared her to Rose. Clearly, beneath her brash exterior Ivy harboured insecurities about her future at Campion's. "I meant, what you think you will be doing next year, or when you're twenty-five or even thirty."

"What do you think I am? A crystal-ball gazer?" scoffed Ivy, as Effie secured the last veil in place. "This time last year I thought I would be dancing in the chorus down the Walworth Road until my knees gave out. In July I wished I'd died in the fire, I was in that much pain. In September I thought I'd never work again because of my rotten scars. And look at me now!

Heading up the bill at Campion's. We none of us know what fate has in store for us."

The music heralding Ivy's entrance began. "All I know is that for the next seven minutes I'm going to go out there and slay 'em. I'm top of the tree at Campion's, and I mean to stay there. Nobody is going to stop me performing at Campion's, and," she put her finger to the side of her nose and looked smug, "I've had offers. Good ones too. But I like it here. It attracts all those classy types. Nobody, not even you, Rose Campion, with your new act and Thomas Campion in your pocket, is going to knock me off my perch."

Rose opened her mouth to protest, but Ivy had flounced away, gliding on to the stage and moving her hips with such sinuous ease that Rose was reminded of a poisonous snake.

5

Rose gazed around Campion's, hugging herself with pleasure. Beneath the orchestra, she could just detect the soft wheeziness of the gas lights, a sound that she thought made it seem as if the very building was alive and breathing. The music hall had never looked more beautiful. The eggshell-blue walls were freshly painted. The gilt mirrors reflected back the delighted faces of the crowd as they watched Ivy – or rather, Desiree – with rapt attention.

Rose slipped back to her seat as soon as Ivy had begun her act, weaving her way through the crowd and the final straggling latecomers. She nodded to several regulars she knew, checked that the Tanner Street boys weren't trying to steal anyone's purse, and told a well-dressed gentleman, who had a stooped, half-veiled lady on his arm, her face turned down to the ground, where they could find a seat at the front of the gallery. A whoop went up from the auditorium as Ivy removed her fourth veil with a dramatic flourish. The girl had a genuine sense of style, thought Rose. Maybe Thomas was wrong about her future prospects.

Ivy sashayed across the stage, removing the sixth veil as she moved. The crowd hollered with pleasure. Rose glanced across at the table where Edward and his party were seated. Grace was clapping with unalloyed pleasure. She saw that Sir Godfrey was no longer in his seat but had moved to the side of the auditorium. His eyes were gleaming, as if he was drinking Ivy in. Perdita Black was absent too, standing a little further forward amid a gaggle of people as if she wanted a closer view. The music swelled, and Ivy began to rotate like a dervish, spinning across the stage as if her life depended on it. Many of the crowd were up on their feet, shouting, "Desiree! Desiree!" over and over as Ivy suddenly spun to a stop. She pulled away the final veil with a swagger to reveal herself demurely dressed in Eastern-style pantaloons, and a glittery blouse that daringly showed a glimpse of midriff. Her beautiful eyes, visible over the small veil that covered the bottom half of her face, were huge and shone seductively.

The audience went mad, yelling their approval and stamping their feet. There was a drum roll and the music began again, and Ivy began to pirouette on the spot. She whirled and twirled, spinning like a dizzying human top as the crowd clapped along as they always did, the sound of five hundred pairs of hands coming together and creating a crack as loud as any pistol shot. Ivy turned 360 degrees, the audience's hands came together again, and just as they did, Ivy suddenly jerked and stumbled unexpectedly, reminding Rose of a juddering wind-up music-box ballerina.

Ivy staggered and lurched towards the side of the stage as if overcome by dizziness. Rose leaned forward. What was wrong with the girl?

Suddenly Rose noticed a small splash of red on the aquamarine material near Ivy's neck. Perhaps Ivy wasn't dizzy from twirling, but because she was hurt? Somehow – Rose couldn't imagine how – she must have injured herself during the dance. Thomas had also realised that something was seriously amiss, and he and Rose raced up on to the stage, just as Ivy's legs buckled beneath her and she toppled into the arms of one of the quick-thinking stagehands, Luke Mumbles, who had stepped out on to the stage just in time to catch her. A great buzz and hum of astonishment rose from the auditorium as, very gently, Luke dragged Ivy out of sight of the audience to the side of the stage. Rose and Thomas knelt down beside her, and Luke put a rolled-up blanket behind her head.

"Some rotter's only gone and shot me," gasped Ivy, sounding quite outraged.

Rose and Thomas looked at each other in consternation. The poor girl must be mistaken. But she had clearly hurt herself in some fashion, and, judging from the increasing amount of blood on her costume, perhaps badly.

"Get Edward, and tell him to get on stage and ask if there is a doctor in the house," ordered Thomas, speaking to Effie, who had flung herself down beside them. "And if there isn't, get Luke to run for Dr Neagle in Tooley Street and tell him it's urgent." Ivy had turned as white as snow.

"Rose," said Thomas. "Can you lift up Ivy's veil a little, please, so we can at least see the wound and try and stem the flow of blood.

Rose did as he ordered, and the source of the bleeding was immediately apparent – a small, round hole at the base of Ivy's neck. Thomas frowned, and signalled to one of the stagehands to bring one of the veils, which he wrapped firmly around Ivy's neck to try and stem the blood loss. Rose held Ivy's hand and stroked it gently. Edward had made his announcement, but to no response, and the orchestra had started playing quietly to appease the crowd. Thomas signalled to Lottie to get the ballet girls on stage. The show always went on, even when there had been an accident.

"The doctor will be here very soon, Ivy. He'll soon patch you up, and you'll be back dancing right as new," said Rose soothingly.

Ivy shook her head sadly. "That bullet had me name on it. It's like I said, Rose, we don't know what fate has in store for us." She had a faraway look in her eyes. "But least I made my mark. Not everyone can say that they were top of the bill at Campion's."

"Not just top of the bill, Ivy," said Thomas gruffly, "but top of the bill for nine weeks solid. That's quite a feat."

Ivy tried to smile. "I was hoping to break the record." Thomas had taken Ivy's other hand. She was clearly finding it difficult to breathe, but she wouldn't be silenced. "I know I haven't been easy to like, but I've liked being at Campion's all right. I've loved it. It's been the best nine weeks of my life."

"You'll be back, Ivy. You'll recover. You'll have another nine weeks at the top. At least. You'll probably break the record," said Thomas.

A tear rolled down Ivy's cheek. "You're just humouring me, Thomas Campion." Ivy's voice was becoming fainter. She smiled weakly at Rose. "I've been such a cow, Rosie. Everyone will be pleased to see the back of me."

Rose squeezed her hand. "Don't be silly, Ivy," she said. "Of course they won't."

Ivy made a sound like a chuckle. "Well, Rose Campion, I must have upset someone good and proper. They've only gone and shot me."

"Ivy," said Rose urgently. "Do you know who could have had a reason to shoot you?"

Ivy gave another chuckle. "Everyone, ducky. You included, Rosie Campion. Way I've behaved over the last nine weeks, there ain't nobody at Campion's who wouldn't want to shoot me if they got the chance. Not even that damn cat, Ophelia, if she could hold a pistol in her paw." She began to laugh. "You can have the tiger cub, Rosie, if you can find her. Call her Ivy. Something to remember me by. Hope that tiger is better tempered than me."

She laughed again, and this time the laughter turned to gasping. Blood began to bubble at the corners of her mouth. She struggled to raise herself up.

"I'd have loved another week top of the bill…" Her voice faded, and she sank back again with her eyes closed, just as the ballet girls launched into the cancan.

Dr Neagle hurried through the stage door, and, spotting his patient at the side of the stage, he knelt down by Ivy and held her wrist, looking for a pulse. He frowned and slipped a small mirror from his pocket and held it against her lips. There was no misting breath. He shook his head and then peered at the wound below her neck. "Bullet went down into the lung by the look of it." Thomas picked up one of Ivy's seven veils and covered her face gently with it. His voice cracked, as he said fiercely, "However Ivy behaved, she didn't deserve this. Who would do such a monstrous thing? Who would shoot a defenceless young woman in cold blood?" He nodded at Luke. "Run to Inspector Cliff at Scotland Yard and tell him to come quickly: there has been a murder at Campion's."

6

It was two days after Ivy's death. Campion's was still closed as a mark of respect and wouldn't reopen until the next day. Ivy had been lowered into the frozen ground in St Olave's churchyard that afternoon amid flurries of snow. The mourners, huddled together against the icy wind, had mostly been from Campion's.

Thomas had been to Ivy's lodgings and spoken to her unhelpful landlady, whose only concern had been for the fact that Ivy was a week behind with her rent, which Thomas paid. He sorted through Ivy's meagre belongings in the hope of discovering a family address, but there was nothing. It appeared that Ivy had either been quite alone in the world, or had cut all ties with her family.

Lottie ensured that the entire chorus turned out for the funeral, arguing that while Ivy had done little to endear herself to them, it would be mean-spirited not to give her a good send-off. Most of the stagehands had turned up. Edward sent a wreath and came in person, and Grace was there too, with Perdita Black beside her. More surprisingly, Sir Godfrey had attended, which rather softened him to Rose. He must have a kind heart, she thought, to come to the funeral of a chorus girl he had never met. He further endeared himself when Grace asked to see Effie's mother's gravestone, and Effie and Rose took the engaged pair to see it. Grace had almost slipped on an icy patch and when she put her hand on Iris Madley's tombstone to steady herself it rocked, revealing a deep hole under the left-hand side.

"We should fill that in before the headstone falls over and cracks," said Sir Godfrey, and he called over one of the gravediggers and watched until it was filled in to his satisfaction. Then he thumped the top of the headstone to ensure it was stable.

The funeral was a glum occasion enlivened only by the moment when Thomas stepped forward to lift the first spadeful of earth on top of the coffin, and the tiger cub – which so far had evaded all attempts at capture – suddenly made an appearance on the wall of the graveyard, and for a moment sat quietly watching, as if paying its final respects. Then it swaggered sleekly along the top of wall with its tail in the air, before jumping down and disappearing from sight. Rose, arm in arm with Aurora and Effie, hoped that the tiger was a female, because when the Zoological Gardens did finally capture the animal she was determined to get Thomas to do everything in his power to ensure that it was named after Ivy.

They had gone to back to Campion's for pies and sandwiches, which Sir Godfrey had insisted on paying for. He had suggested that anything left over should be distributed to the mudlark children.

"Those poor little mites," he said, "out by the river in all weathers. It breaks my heart to think of them."

He had only stayed a few minutes more, apologising as he hurried away, saying he had unexpected urgent business to attend to arising from one of the charity committees he sat on in the seaside towns of Margate, Herne Bay and Whitstable on the Kent coast. He would be away for some time, returning only in time for the dinner in Grace's honour before the wedding. He had kissed Grace's hand as he bade goodbye and said, kindly but – Rose couldn't help thinking – rather pompously, "Goodbye, my dear. Enjoy yourself – and do not forget that on Boxing Day you will become Lady Caskins."

Rose caught Perdita's eye. There was something in the way that Perdita gazed at Sir Godfrey that made Rose murmur wickedly, "It's not as if as soon as he's left, Grace is going to leap on the trapeze and hang upside down showing everyone her knickerbockers. Although I'd love it if she did."

Perdita suppressed a grin. "Sir Godfrey is a man who sets great store by his reputation and good name."

"But good name aside," asked Rose, "is he also a good man?"

Perdita replied quickly. "He is a very charitable one by all accounts, and he always treats Grace with kindness."

Rose felt relieved. Sir Godfrey may seem a little stuffy, but kindness went a long way.

Without Thomas taking her in as a baby, Rose would probably have died. More than anyone, she knew the value of kindness.

"Are you named after Shakespeare's heroine in *The Winter's Tale*?" Rose asked, changing the subject.

"Yes," said Perdita softly. "For my sins, I am. Did you know Shakespeare made the name up? It means 'the lost one'," she said, and a faraway look came into her eye.

"It's such a pretty name," said Rose.

"And you, Rose, are a real-life Perdita, or so I hear from Rory. I don't know why Thomas didn't think of calling you that, given his love of Shakespeare and the way he found you abandoned as a tiny baby."

Rose laughed. "Probably because he didn't plan to bring me up as a shepherdess in Southwark and was confident that I wasn't a real-life princess."

Perdita smiled. "But Aurora turned out to be a lady. So why shouldn't you be a princess?"

Rose made a face. "I'd hate that. It must be awful being a princess. All that bowing and curtseying and never being able to climb on to a roof when you want."

"Grace told me that you've been searching for your mother but that the trail has gone stone cold. You should never give up on your dream of finding her, Rose. "

"Oh, but I haven't given up," said Rose fiercely. "I won't give up until I find her, or know for certain that she is dead. Because I don't believe she would give up on me."

Perdita looked sad, and Rose wondered whether she too had lost someone in her life.

"I hope you find your mother eventually," said Perdita, before making her excuses and joining Grace's side.

* ✳ *

It was later in the day and Rose, Thomas, Edward, Aurora and Effie were seated around the table in Thomas's study with Inspector Cliff and his assistant, Billy Proctor. A copy of *The Stage* lay on the table, its headline screaming: "Desiree dead in on-stage shooting." They all knew Inspector Cliff well. He had investigated the theft of the Doomstone from Campion's and the murder of the magician Gandini. Although he had proved himself rather bumbling in many regards – at one point even arresting Effie for Gandini's murder – he was a likeable man. As Rose was fond of saying, he always did his best, even if his best sometimes turned out to be inadequate.

"The bullet could have been fired from anywhere in the hall," said Cliff. "It wouldn't be hard to conceal a small pistol. It makes my job all the more difficult. We couldn't detain everyone present at Campion's on the night Ivy was shot, and by the time my men and I arrived, many had left, and the murderer almost certainly slipped away in the crowd. Our only real hope is to discover the motive for killing Ivy and hope that leads us to her killer." He paused and looked around the table.

"I know from what I've been told that Ivy hadn't endeared herself to her fellow performers here at Campion's, but everyone protests their innocence and appears to have alibis. Of course, we will be cross-checking those alibis very carefully."

"I find it hard to believe that anyone at Campion's killed Ivy," said Thomas. "It would have been difficult for someone connected with the theatre to slip into the auditorium completely unseen. Somebody – the bar staff or the box-office staff – would likely as not spot them. It would be a risky strategy. Unless people are colluding with each other to provide alibis."

Inspector Cliff nodded. "Quite so. Maybe they are. It's clear that most people working at Campion's held a grudge against Ivy, and a grudge is always a reason to kill."

Rose frowned. "Look, Inspector," she said. "Nobody liked Ivy very much, but that doesn't mean they wanted to murder her, even if they joked out loud about it. Hall folk are used to dealing with prima donnas. There are feuds and fights all the time over who has got top billing or the better dressing room, or who the crowd likes best. Even who is getting paid what. Ivy was unpopular, but we've had plenty of acts here at Campion's who have behaved worse, and they haven't ended up dead on stage like Ivy Puddlewick."

"But Ivy did die, and unless there's a madman out there taking potshots at music-hall stars, she died for a reason," said the Inspector. "Whoever shot her was a fine marksman. They were dead on target from some distance. The gun had to be fired at the very moment that the audience were clapping to cover the sound. That requires real expertise. Somebody must have seen something.

What surprises me is that nobody has come forward as a witness."

"It shouldn't do," said Rose. "After all, the Doomstone was stolen in full view of five hundred people and nobody noticed. It's the same with poor Ivy. Nobody saw someone pull a pistol because they were all fixated on her dancing. Done discreetly enough, whoever was responsible would have an excellent chance of avoiding being spotted."

The Inspector nodded. "Can any of you think of anything unusual that's happened over the last few days or weeks?"

"There was the tiger," said Effie excitedly.

Inspector Cliff smiled and put his hand up to stop her. "Except the tiger. Everyone, without fail, has told me about the tiger cub. And the note attached. It's intriguing, I agree, particularly the way Ivy is referred to as a tiger and the writer calls themselves a tiger hunter. I would like to find whoever sent the note and the animal. But I have a hunch that the reason Ivy was killed lies at Campion's. Somebody wanted to get rid of Ivy. The question is, why?"

The Inspector stood up and turned to Edward. "I have appointments tomorrow to interview everyone who was in your party, sir."

"I bet some of them aren't at all happy about the police turning up on their doorsteps," said Rose.

"Some have made that quite clear," replied the Inspector. "But I intend to find Ivy's murderer, and whether they are a pauper or a toff I will bring them to justice. It is the least that Ivy deserves."

Everyone stood up and Edward and Aurora left to go back to Silver Square. Thomas and Rose and Effie lingered for a little with the Inspector.

"I have some news for you all. The Duchess has been released from prison."

Effie's eyes darkened with fear. She had met the Duchess before, when they had both been incarcerated in Holloway prison, and she had been chilled by her ruthlessness.

Cliff continued. "I'm afraid those crooked lawyers of hers found a legal loophole that got her released. I'm sure she is no threat to any of you at all, but I thought I would mention it as both of you, Rose and Effie, had some contact with her, and she was always so interested in Campion's."

"But surely that was only because of the

Gandini connection?" asked Rose.

"That's probably the case," said the Inspector. "But I thought I'd mention it in case there is anything more to it."

There was something about the look on his face that made Rose feel certain he was hiding something.

"There *is* something else. What is it?" she demanded.

Cliff hesitated for a moment.

"As I said, the Duchess was released because of a legal loophole, and perhaps because she has a hold over some people in high places. But in the process of the negotiations for her release, Billy visited her several times in Holloway. Of course, the Duchess will always try to manipulate people for her own ends. She'd betray her own flesh and blood if she thought there was an advantage to be gained. But during their conversations, the Duchess did tell Billy that Lizzie Gawkin, the woman who we know stole you as a baby, Rose, occasionally did small jobs for her. Petty stuff. Nothing significant."

Rose felt a prickle down her spine. She saw Thomas become more alert.

"So do you think she might know who my

mother was? Is?" asked Rose. The words came out croaky because her mouth was so dry.

"I'm afraid I can't say," said the Inspector. "It's why I hadn't planned to say anything at this stage. But Billy thinks she almost certainly has more information than she is letting on."

Billy Proctor nodded.

"At the very least, she may know from outside which London theatre you were snatched. If we had that information, even with the time that has elapsed, we would have a far greater chance of discovering the identity of your mother. I suspect she does know. She never forgets a face or a piece of information that she thinks may be of use to her in the future. If your mother is still alive, I reckon the Duchess may know who she is and where we might find her. Whatever happens, we're going to be keeping a close eye on her. She was a close associate of Ambrose Skelly before her arrest. We hope she may lead us to him."

Rose felt her stomach tighten. She wasn't sure if she felt excited by the news or anxious. She felt a strong urge to wrap her arms around Thomas and hug him.

"Ambrose Skelly? The Cobra?" asked Effie

excitedly, who, since she had learned to read, had become an avid reader of the more sensational stories in *The Illustrated Crime News*. "The theory is that he skipped to France and is living the high life in Monte Carlo. Has *Crime News* got it wrong, Inspector?"

The Inspector smiled. He had a soft spot for Effie, which Rose suspected was well oiled by guilt after he had mistakenly arrested Effie for the murder of Gandini. She would still be languishing in Holloway prison today if it had not been for Rose's determination to prove her friend innocent.

"Maybe he is in Monte Carlo," said Inspector Cliff, "but I rather doubt it. We had all the ports watched. My hunch is that he's lying low somewhere. I only wish I knew where. I can't help feeling that he's somewhere under our noses and we just can't see him. That's why we're trying to keep an eye on the Duchess, though she's a slippery character and a mistress of disguise. But I just can't help feeling that the two of them might try to make an alliance. Although of course if it ever came down to it, one would betray the other without the slightest qualm if it suited them."

After Thomas had seen the Inspector and Billy Proctor down to the door he came back up to his study to find Rose sitting quite alone. He took one of her hands.

"Rose," he said gently. "I know how much you want to find your mother, and if the Inspector does get more information, you know I will support you in your search, wherever that might lead."

Rose looked into Thomas's kind, gentle face. She knew that he was telling her that even if finding her mother took her away from him, he would bear it for her sake. His generosity made her want to weep.

"I know you will, Thomas. I have never doubted it."

7

Rose and Effie walked along Lant Street in the direction of Campion's with a skip in their step. Snowflakes danced around their faces in the darkness. Some of the small terraced houses already had wreaths made out of holly on their doors for Christmas. Although Inspector Cliff appeared to have made no further progress in his investigation, and the atmosphere at Campion's was a little odd, as if everyone was eyeing each other up as a potential murder suspect, they were both looking forward to tonight. Madame Elenora de Valentina was making her debut, and Pru Smith – or rather, Belle Canterbury – was also back on the bill.

Over her arm, Rose was carrying the sailor suit that Pru would wear for the act, transforming her from shy, plain Prudence Smith into a fragile, handsome young man who sang hauntingly beautiful love songs. Pru's mother, now fully recovered, had been making some last-minute alterations to the suit – Pru had lost weight and the trousers needed taking in. Rose and Effie had sat chatting to her as the old lady wielded her needle and thread.

"I'm so sorry I haven't got this ready and waiting for you," said Mrs Smith in her thick Italian accent. "I was delayed. While Prudencia was rehearsing this afternoon, I had a visitor. An old lady who used to live in this house before my poor husband and I moved here. That was before Prudencia was born. She just wanted to have a peep inside. She was very nice. It brought back so many memories of when Prudencia was just a little girl."

"Why don't you come back with us to Campion's and watch Pru tonight? It's cold out, but not too bitter," said Rose.

Mrs Smith shook her head vigorously and laughed.

"It is not this cold I fear. My lovely Prudencia would murder me if she knew I watch her on her first night back on the bill. She says I gives her the stage fright." She threw her arms up into the air in mock outrage. "What a thing to say about her poor mama. I will stay here by the fire. I will come see her in a few days when the nerves are settled. I would like to see this Madame de Valentina too. My Prudencia said she met her at the theatre this morning where Madame de Valentina was preparing. She said that Madame was very charming. She apologised for taking top billing." Mrs Smith sniffed. "I don't like to speak ill of the dead, but that Ivy woman, she only ever sneered at my Prudencia."

Rose and Effie said goodbye to Mrs Smith and set off back to Campion's, keeping their eyes peeled for the tiger cub, still on the loose despite numerous sightings. There were rumours that the Tanner Street boys had been out doing a spot of tiger-hunting. Rose hoped for the tiger's sake that they were not successful.

The churchyard was a place that made Effie feel nervous after dark, as if danger might loom up any minute from out of the shadows, but she could see that Rose was itching to go and see if the tiger was there, so she suggested that they make a short detour to St Olave's graveyard in case they could glimpse it. Entering through the back gate as quietly as they could, they were rewarded almost immediately with a sudden flash of black stripes and reddish fur emerging from dense bushes and disappearing over the far wall. Rose felt relief. Clearly the Tanner Street boys hadn't trapped the tiger – at least, not yet.

They turned to head back to Campion's, just as the moon came out. Effie suddenly stiffened, nudged Rose and put her finger to her mouth. Over in the far corner of the graveyard, two figures – both cloaked and hooded – stood with their backs to them, whispering together. They were so close to Effie's mother's grave they were almost standing on it. The conversation appeared to come to a close. One of the figures – they couldn't see if it was a man or a woman – glided down the pathway towards the side gate, moving as silently and effortlessly as a ghost. The remaining figure turned slightly, as if making to leave by the main gate, giving a glimpse of a partial profile. Effie suppressed a gasp. The woman looked sharply around, as if she had heard something, and Rose pulled Effie down behind a mausoleum erected in memory of a spice merchant.

Rose's heart stuttered. She understood now

why Effie had gasped. It was the Duchess. She was sure of it. She signalled to Effie to remain silent, and then very carefully she peeped out from behind the gravestone. The Duchess was peering suspiciously into the shadows. Then, clearly satisfied, she straightened up and picked her way through the weeping angels and crooked gravestones until she reached the churchyard path, and headed purposefully towards the river. Rose and Effie waited a moment and then set off towards Campion's at a run, almost bumping into Perdita, who was hurrying ahead of them in the same direction, warmly wrapped in a thick, dark cloak.

By the time Rose and Effie arrived back, Campion's was already busy, and queues were beginning to form. Nobody wanted to miss Madame de Valentina's Campion's debut. A woman, ill defended against the cold, stood alone outside the hall, gazing at the poster for the performance as if her eyes were trying to drink it in.

The girls went straight up to Thomas's office, where they told him about spotting both the tiger and the Duchess in the graveyard.

"You don't think the Duchess might have

something to do with Ivy's death?" asked Rose.

"Why do you think that, Rose?" asked Thomas, and Rose shrugged. She couldn't think of a single reason why an underworld criminal would want to kill Ivy Puddlewick.

"Like the Inspector, I imagine the reason for Ivy's murder lies rather closer to home," said Thomas. "But I will send a note to Inspector Cliff to tell him that you saw her close to Campion's. She must have a reason to be in this part of town. The East End is her usual patch." His brow furrowed, and Rose wondered if Thomas was more worried than he was letting on. Thomas said he would also get in contact with the zoo again about the tiger.

"You should," said Effie. "It's getting much bigger. It might gobble somebody up quite soon."

"Or get skinned by the Tanner Street boys," said Rose darkly.

Lottie poked her head around the door. "Bad news. A message has come from Susan – she's down with influenza, so you haven't got a pot girl tonight, and with three of them off sick in the kitchen, it's going to be all hands on deck."

Rose stood up with a sigh.

"I'd better go down and lend them a hand. I

had hoped to see Madame de Valentina make her debut, but it looks like I'll be scrubbing pots in the kitchen."

"Sorry, Rosie," said Thomas ruefully. "I'll try and make it up to you."

From the kitchen, Rose, up to her arms in water, trying to make a dent in the piles of dirty pots and crockery, could hear that Campion's was buzzing in anticipation of the debut of Madame de Valentina. Effie had come and helped scrub plates for twenty minutes before being called backstage to help, and even Aurora, who had arrived with a party from Silver Square, appeared at the kitchen door and made to roll up her silk sleeves and lend a hand. Rose had chased her away.

"Come off it, Rory," said Rose. "The place will be crawling with journalists come to see the woman who has replaced poor Ivy at the top of the bill, and no doubt hoping for yet another murder on the Campion's stage. If they get wind that a Lord's daughter is working as a pot girl in the kitchen, they will turn it into a scandal and drag the Easingford name through the mud. It's unfair on Grace. Sir Godfrey wouldn't like it at all. Anyway, your dress will be ruined, and

I might want to borrow it for that posh dinner when Grace gets given those emeralds."

Aurora retreated reluctantly, promising to look out for evening frocks for Rose and Effie.

Rose set to work on yet another pie dish. The burned remnants of a beef and oyster pie stubbornly resisted her efforts. Her fingers and knuckles were red and raw. It wouldn't be long before Madame de Valentina was on stage. She rubbed her sleeve across her sweaty forehead. The stack of pots and baking trays and pie dishes was still mounting at an alarming rate. She needed to cool down. She removed her apron and slipped out of the kitchen door into the icy air outside. It was snowing again. Rose luxuriated in the feeling of cool snow melting on her hot forehead. She closed her eyes for a moment, and when she opened them again, a woman was standing a few steps away, her eyes fixed on Rose.

"I'm sorry to bother you," she said. "I wondered if there was any work in the kitchen tonight?"

Rose looked at the woman in surprise. She spoke with an educated voice, and although the washed-out outfit that she was wearing had seen far better days, it had clearly once been stylish. The woman had a nasty gash over her eye, her face was grey with tiredness, and her matted chestnut hair was tied back with an old bootlace. Rose thought it might be the same women she had seen hanging around outside the theatre earlier, staring at the poster of Madame de Valentina.

"I just need a chance to get back on my feet," continued the woman. "I'm not afraid of hard work."

From beyond the kitchen came the roar of the crowd. Rose cast a longing glance backwards. She would love to be out in the hall tonight rather than scraping pots.

"Do you have any experience washing pots?" she asked.

The woman shook her head nervously. "But I'm a quick learner." And then she added, with a dash of spirit and irony that endeared her to Rose, "Being a pot girl can't be that difficult."

Rose smiled. "No, it's not difficult, but it is very hard work."

"I've plenty of elbow grease," said the woman ruefully, holding up her elbow and showing where the once-fine blue material was soiled with dark oil.

The attempt at a joke made Rose smile. For a moment she gazed at the woman again, and the woman held her stare with grey eyes, dark as slate. Rose said, "Well, we could certainly do with a hand if you're willing. I can pay you, and you are welcome to as many pies as you can eat."

"I can't thank you enough. You're my fairy godmother."

"Actually," said Rose, "I think you might be mine. You've saved me from a night in the kitchen."

* ✳ *

It was less than half an hour before she joined Effie and Aurora, who were sharing a banquette at the back of the hall near the bar. The woman, who had said her name was Ella, had turned out to be a real grafter, and within twenty minutes of arriving she had made a significant dent in the pile of dirty pots.

"Shove up," said Rose, as she slipped in beside them and explained her good fortune and the miraculous arrival of the woman. "Madame de Valentina will be on after Pru does her act, and I want to see if her world domination extends to quieting a rowdy Campion's audience."

The theatre was buzzing. Notoriety had brought half of Southwark and Bermondsey out, as well as plenty of more affluent punters from the West End.

Effie grinned. "Maybe she'll read your mind, Rosie."

Rose snorted. "If she tries, she'll find it a complete blank."

"Don't tell me you are doubting Madame de Valentina's remarkable talents, Rosie?" Effie said, picking up a playbill and pointing at the lettering. "Look! It says 'ere, she's the 'Wonder of the Age'. It's written down in black and white so it must be true. One of the things I've noticed since I learned to read is that people believe things when they're written down. Even complete lies."

"Well, Thomas clearly isn't completely convinced about Madame de Valentina – he's only booked her for tonight," said Rose. "He doesn't want his fingers burned again after those useless illusionists, Hopkin and Dent. They turned out to be such a disappointment on Tuesday – they were as nervous as cats, fumbling their illusions so badly. I can't imagine why they were ever rated so highly. He had to pay them off for the entire week – if he let them go on stage again the Campion's audience would have murdered them." She stopped and put a hand to her mouth, realising what she had said and how inappropriate it was, after what had happened to poor Ivy. Somebody in the audience *had* murdered her – but not because her act was bad.

"Well, I've heard Madame de Valentina is really very impressive," said Rory. "That she knows things about people that they have never told a living soul."

Rose frowned. "Honestly, Rory, you don't actually believe this stuff, do you?"

"Of course not," she said indignantly. "I know it's just an act. But she's all the rage. Georgiana Fitzcillian said she was astonishing. She saw her on Friday night at the Alhambra. She told me all about it when we went to her house for tea this afternoon. Apparently two of the Fitzcillian parlourmaids went, and one of them, Polly, was hypnotised and barked like a dog, and the other got told she would come into money, and the next day she found a shilling."

"Georgiana Fitzcillian is a nincompoop," said Rose. "When she saw Effie performing she was convinced that she was doing real magic. The shilling was a coincidence."

Effie gave Rose a warning look and Rory swallowed hard.

"Well, I was just reporting what I'd heard," said Rory defensively.

Rose gave an inward sigh. She could kick herself for not keeping her big mouth shut. Only this afternoon Effie had warned her that she was going to drive a wedge between herself and Aurora if she kept on sniping at her aristocratic connections. Rose couldn't wait until Grace and Sir Godfrey got married, and everything got back to normal – including her and Rory doing the new bicycle act. Maybe Aurora could be persuaded to take part in the pantomime after all. She squeezed Rory's hand tightly.

"Of course you're right, Rory. I'm being horrid. Don't listen to me. Madame de Valentina probably is the eighth wonder of the world. I hope so, for Thomas's sake."

Edward and Grace arrived just before Belle Canterbury took to the stage, and joined Perdita, who was sitting at a small table, drumming her fingers and seeming nervous. Rose went over to talk to them.

"Are you looking forward to seeing Madame de Valentina?" she asked Perdita, who seemed jumpy and distracted.

"Yes, of course," said Perdita. "I can't wait to get a good look at her." There was a quaver in her voice.

Pru's angelic voice rose to the rafters, its ethereal beauty wrapping the entire audience in a cloak of emotion. Dressed in the sailor suit, she sang yearningly of a love lost forever. Rose could hear the sound of soft sobbing all around the auditorium, and when she glanced at Perdita's face, she saw that her eyes were dark pools of tears. Even Thomas, who had heard the song many times, looked moved, as if remembering his own lost wife, Maud, and twin baby daughters, who had all succumbed to the measles, turning him from a proud and loving father and husband into a grief-stricken widower in less than a week. Thomas often said that if he had not found Rose abandoned on the steps of Campion's so soon after their deaths, he would never have survived his loss.

Pru was taking her bow, and Rose knew that within minutes she would have wiped the make-up from her face, changed back into her skirts, reattached the false plait she wore when out of doors, put her hat on her head and slipped out of the Campion's stage door. Before St Olave's had chimed the quarter she would be back by her mother's side in Lant Street.

The ballet girls were back on stage doing their Little Bo Peep act, but few of the audience were taking much notice. They were getting drinks and chatting excitedly in readiness for the main event: Madame de Valentina. The lights flickered. Then came the distant, silvery tinkle of a small bell, sounding eerie in the darkness. Suddenly a light appeared from out of the darkness and darted about the stage like a little bird. The crowd, already in a heightened state of excitement, squealed. Rose smiled. It wasn't a difficult trick to pull off, but it was mightily effective. The bell sounded again, and as a haze of blue smoke cleared, the light found the face of Madame de Valentina, so for a moment she looked like a disembodied head suspended in mid-air, dark eyes simmering in an unnaturally white face. The crowd gasped. Even Rose felt a shiver down her spine. She leaned forward and felt a strange sense of dread, as if something terrible was about to happen.

Madame de Valentina emerged out of the darkness into a pool of light. She was a commanding figure, dressed in a long silvery dress that glittered in the lights. Her arms were sheathed in black silk gloves that extended almost to her shoulders. Her eyes glittered in her snow-white face, her blonde hair was pulled back severely and piled on her head, and her cheekbones gleamed in a way that reminded Rose of the Snow Queen, a character in a story she had read in a book of Danish fairy tales that Thomas had given her. There were two tables and a chair on stage. On one of the tables sat a crystal ball and a small silver bell, and on the other a cauldron from which wreathes of smoke coiled.

Rose nudged Thomas and whispered, "I think someone's been reading too much *Macbeth*."

Madame de Valentina couldn't have possibly heard her, but Rose felt as if the woman's eyes had sought her out and were boring into her. It was ridiculous, of course, but it still made her shift uncomfortably in her chair.

Madame de Valentina began to speak, her voice low and a touch husky. What followed were fifteen minutes of mind-reading tricks, cleverly delivered but of a kind that were regularly seen in music halls across the land. Rose winked at Effie. She knew that Effie could perform tricks as well as this, persuading the punters that they had freely chosen a particular card or circled a word in a book when in fact they had been cleverly directed to make the right choice. Rose glanced around. All of Perdita's nervous tension seemed to have dissipated, and she sat relaxed alongside Grace and Edward.

Just as Rose was beginning to think that things couldn't get duller, Madame de Valentina suddenly changed tack. She held a hand in the air to quieten the crowd and gazed around the auditorium, her head on one side like an inquisitive bird. She scanned the audience, occasionally capturing an individual in her gaze and scrutinising them long and hard. Rose caught Thomas's eye. It was a good act, creating suspense because it was unnerving, but both of them knew that any really talented actor could do the same. Some performers had a talent for holding an audience in the palm of their hand, and Madame de Valentina was clearly one of them. She continued to fix the audience with her dagger-like eyes. The entire room was still now, as if every single person was holding their breath. The silence was suddenly broken by the nervous giggle of several young women, including one with red hair sitting a few rows back and to the side of the auditorium.

Madame de Valentina swung round towards her, pointed a long finger at the girl and said, "Florrie? It *is* Florrie, isn't it?"

The young woman's eyes bulged with surprise as she nodded. She looked terrified. "How ... how..." she stuttered. "How do you know my name?"

"Because her mind rules the world," whispered Rose, and Effie and Aurora giggled. Thomas frowned, and Madame de Valentina swivelled round and gave Rose a glare that was worthy of Medusa.

Madame de Valentina turned back to Florrie.

"Don't be scared, my dear. Come up here – and why don't you bring Col with you?"

Florrie and Col, the young man next to her, looked at each other, perplexed. How did she know their names? Madame de Valentina beckoned them towards her. They stood on the stage beside her, looking awkward, as if willing the ground to open up and swallow them.

"Now, I know that you two have some delightful news that I think you should share with everyone."

Florrie and Col's eyes were almost popping out of their heads.

"You can't know that," whispered Col.

"We ain't told nobody. Not even me mum. It were only on the way 'ere it happened," said Florrie.

"Ah, yes," said Madame de Valentina softly, and there was a tender smile on her face, "and the 'it' you refer to is Col asking you to marry him, and you, Florrie, saying yes, isn't it?"

There was a cheer and round of applause from the crowd. It was clear, from the way Florrie and Col were gawping at her, that Madame de

Valentina was correct.

"They're a plant," came a cry from the audience. "It's all a set-up." It was one of the Tanner Street boys – not Campion's most popular regulars.

Madame de Valentina gazed at him for a second, and then she smiled and said smoothly, "If you think I'm a fake that's entirely up to you, John. But if you are going to go around making accusations, I will have to tell everybody about the whiskered old man whose pocketwatch you filched on London Bridge this afternoon, and about the—"

"All right, all right, I'll keep me trap shut, just don't say another word," screeched John, astonishment and panic rising in his voice. The audience, particularly the Southwark locals, roared with laughter, delighted to see one of the bullying, swaggering Tanner Street boys cut down to size.

"Where was I, before I was so rudely interrupted?" asked Madame de Valentina.

Rose had to admire her composure and the way she had got the audience onside. It was a real art. Madame turned back to Florrie and Col, and smiled kindly.

"Why don't you tell the audience a little about

yourselves. Don't be shy."

Florrie looked at Col, who nodded.

"We're nuffing special," said Florrie. "Col and me both work at Lady Plockton's in St James' Square. I'm the scullery maid and Col was the stable boy, but Mr Hoppity said he was wasted there and now he's the tea boy. My Col's got prospects," she said, and with such pride that Rose thought that nobody couldn't be touched by the girl's sincerity.

Madame de Valentina turned to Col.

"Col, will you show us how you proposed to Florrie?"

He shook his head vigorously.

"Go on, Col," said Florrie shyly.

He shook his head again.

"Would you like me to help you relax?" asked Madame de Valentina.

Col hesitated, but Florrie nodded enthusiastically.

"Both of you, look at me," said Madame. "I will count to ten, and when I ring this bell we will see the proposal." She counted slowly and she rang the bell. The noise was so pure and penetrating it made Rose shiver.

Immediately Col got down on one knee, seized

Florrie's hand and said, "Oh, Florrie, I can't live without you. I know I'm not much of a catch, but will you marry me?"

Florrie's face was shining. "Yes, Col. I will."

The audience clapped and cheered. But the couple didn't move. It was as if they had been turned to stone. Rose leaned forward. It was very odd – she had never seen anything like it. It was as if Florrie and Col were entirely under Madame's control. She whispered something in both their ears that the audience couldn't hear.

"Col," ordered Madame, "come and sit on this chair." The lad complied. "Now Col, you will try and stand up, but you will find yourself unable to do so." The boy tried to stand up but he couldn't. He squirmed and exerted himself until he was red in the face, and the audience guffawed as he redoubled his efforts to no avail.

"Florrie," said Madame. "I would like to see you hop around the stage like a rabbit."

Florrie began hopping, her eyes glazed, and a sweet, almost beatific smile on her face. The audience fell about, but Rose felt uncomfortable. It didn't feel right to be laughing at this sweet, trusting pair, who had no idea of the spectacle they were providing. But she was in the minority.

Most people were laughing heartily, and even Edward and Grace were smiling. She caught Perdita's eye. She looked grave. But they were the two exceptions. None too soon for Rose, Madame de Valentina whispered something else in Florrie's ear, the girl nodded at her, and de Valentina rang the little silver bell. It was as if Florrie and Col had both been awoken from a deep sleep. They stood, looking dazed, on stage, while Madame encouraged the audience to clap the pair and then directed them back to their seats. Both of them were beaming. Rose wondered whether they would be smiling so freely if they knew that they had been made such figures of fun. But perhaps she was being ridiculous for having such qualms. All around them, people were cheering and clapping Florrie and Col on the back.

Perhaps for Florrie and Col this was the one chance they would ever have in their lives to be the centre of attention. Maybe when they were very old they would still be talking about the night they were on stage at Campion's. There was no harm done. The audience had enjoyed it, but Rose wasn't sure the act was good enough to keep Elenora de Valentina at the top of the bill for more than a week or two.

But Madame de Valentina was not finished. The stage was once again wreathed in smoke. The lights lowered, leaving de Valentina looking like a shadowy, almost ghost-like figure in the gloom. A single violin began to play, the sound drifting eerily around the auditorium. Madame de Valentina stepped forward. She placed her palms against her forehead for a moment, then she opened her eyes.

"The spirits are with us tonight," she said, and her voice sounded even more gravelly. The crowd gave a coo of excitement and leaned forward. The sound from the violin grew more haunting. Madame de Valentina began to shake, as if a tremor was passing through her body from top to toe. Then she spoke.

"I have a message from Daniel, who very recently passed over, for his mother or sister. Is there anyone here who knows Daniel?"

There was a charged silence. The crowd shifted expectantly, but nobody spoke. Madame de Valentina was already moving on.

"I have a message, a message from Uncle Jack..." A ripple ran around the crowd. Rose looked at Effie and raised an eyebrow. There would be plenty of people in the audience who had an Uncle Jack. It was a fair bet on Madame de Valentina's part. "The message is for Maisie." She paused and there was no response. "Or perhaps I am mistaken; his voice is very weak. No, no, I think it's for Margie… Or is there a Millie or a Margaret in the audience, with an uncle called Jack who recently passed over?"

"Me, the message is for me! I'm Maggie," cried a thin, careworn woman in the gallery. "We buried Jack last week in St Olave's."

"Yes! Yes! I can hear more clearly now. The message is definitely for Maggie," said Madame de Valentina. "Jack wants you to know that everything will be all right. Your troubles will pass, and he is watching over you and the children, little Meggie and Joey."

Tears were running down the woman's face. "Thank you, oh thank you," she cried, and her sobs carried across the auditorium.

The violin music began again, and another tremor passed through Madame de Valentina's body.

"I can see a spirit in the gallery. Someone connected with Campion's, I believe."

A murmur of excitement passed around the

theatre. Rose glanced up into the gallery. She was certain that she had once seen the ghost of Grace's husband, Ned, there. But she could see nothing now except a sea of expectant faces mesmerised by Madame de Valentina. Judging by the excitement she was generating, Thomas would likely as not be booking her for the rest of the week the very moment she came off stage. She was going to be top of the bill at Campion's for weeks to come, beating poor Ivy's run for sure.

"The message," said Madame de Valentina, "is for Grace, who is, I believe, this gentleman's widow. His name is Ned."

"That's me," squeaked Grace, looking astounded.

"He is telling me that you must follow your heart's desire, Grace. Be guided by your heart, not by expectation. Do not be deceived by appearances."

Madame de Valentina pressed on.

"I have a message for Thomas from Maud," she said.

Rose felt Thomas stiffen beside her. He was looking straight ahead, his face expressionless. Maud was the name of Thomas's dearly beloved dead wife.

"She wants you to know that you are not to blame, and you should forgive yourself for not being there when she and the twins passed over."

Rose saw Thomas's shoulders heave; his face was white with shock. She took his hand and squeezed it tight, and he squeezed it hard back. Effie, Aurora, Edward and Grace, who all knew of Thomas's loss, were looking at him, concern on their faces. Rose felt anger bubbling up inside her. She wanted to end this charade, stop this woman making capital out of other people's misery for entertainment. She didn't know how she was doing it, but she was certain it was some form of fakery. But Madame de Valentina had moved on again. The crowd were hanging on every word.

"I have another message from the other side. This time it is for Effie. It's your mother, Iris. She wants me to tell you how much she loves you. But I must be quick. I have a restless spirit here with a message for Belle..." She paused and frowned. "This is very confusing – the message seems to be for someone who might be called Belle, but who might be called Prudence."

Rose and the others all looked at each other.

Madame de Valentina continued. "It is from your mama. She wants you to keep singing. And she has left something for you, in the secret place that only you two know."

"Well," said Rose loudly, unable to contain herself any more. "This is ridiculous. Effie and I saw Mrs Smith less than two hours ago, and she was as fit as a fiddle."

But the words had barely fallen from her lips when there was a sudden commotion at the door and Prudence rushed in, hatless and coatless, her face streaked with tears.

"It's mama! My poor mama. She's dead! She's dead!"

9

It had taken all of Thomas's authority to quieten the crowd and, eventually, get them to leave. Several audience members had tried to storm the stage, demanding to know if Madame de Valentina could give them messages from their dead loved ones. Only when Thomas had spoken to Madame de Valentina and assured them that she would be on the bill tomorrow, and for at least the next two weeks, had the crowds finally gone home and the doors been closed. Elenora de Valentina hurried away too. She had looked unsettled and seemed upset, brushing aside Rose's offer to find her a hansom cab, as if she wanted to be as far away from Campion's as quickly as possible.

As soon as they could, Thomas, Rose and Effie

hurried to Lant Street, where Edward, Grace, Aurora and Lottie had gone on in advance with Pru. By the time Rose and Thomas reached the house, the undertaker had already arrived and taken the body upstairs to be washed. Pru was quietly sobbing in the chair where her mother had always sat.

"What happened, Pru?" asked Thomas gently.

Prudence sniffed. "I came back from the theatre as usual. Ma had left the back door open as she always does when she knows I'm not doing two shows and she'll still be up. I take a short cut that brings me into the alley that runs behind the yard. It's quicker." She gave a sob. "I spotted that tiger on the way back. Just a tiny glimpse, which gave me a bit of a fright, but it took no notice of me. Mama was pleased to see me back so early. She was sitting in this very chair knitting, looking very spry. I went out in the scullery to make tea, and when I came back she got me to tell her everything about my performance. She said how proud she was of me. She was just telling me about how she had once sung on a stage in Italy when she was a girl, when there was a knock on the front door. It was strange at that time of night, but I went to answer. A woman was there, a shawl over her head. Ever so polite. She had got the right number house but on the wrong street, and I had to give her directions to a couple of streets further down. It took a few moments because she kept repeating the directions back to me and getting them wrong. When I went back into the parlour, Ma was lying on the floor, her face deep in her cushion. There was no breath in her." Pru broke off and gave a sob. "She was dead. I turned her over and her lips were tinged blue. She looked so peaceful."

"And there was nothing else strange?" asked Rose.

Pru shook her head. Then she frowned. "Just a slightly sweet cloying smell. I was only gone a few minutes. If only I hadn't spent so long talking to the woman at the door, I would have been there when she fell! She must have collapsed face down on a cushion. It sucked the breath out of her." Pru broke into a crescendo of sobbing.

"I've sent for Dr Neagle," said Edward. "He said that the old lady's heart must have given out, weakened by her recent illness. She was probably dead before she hit the ground." Then he said, more quietly so the sobbing Pru couldn't hear, "But falling on to the cushion was unlucky. It meant the old lady had no chance. Even if the heart attack didn't kill her, the cushion did the rest. She would have suffocated."

"But she seemed so alive," said Effie, "when Rose and I were here earlier. She was blooming. Rose even said on the way back she hadn't seen Mrs Smith look so well for years."

"Dr Neagle didn't seem surprised," said Edward. "He has attended her for many years and knew her well."

"Pru," asked Rose softly. "You didn't hear your mother fall?"

Pru shook her head.

"What did you do after you realised your mother had died?"

"I ran straight to Campion's and all of you. It was instinct. I was in a daze. There was nowhere else I'd have thought to go. If I'd believed there was any hope, I'd have gone to the neighbours to get them to send for the doctor. But I knew Mama was dead, so I just ran blindly through the streets to Campion's. I didn't even stop for my hat and coat. It was like running to my family."

"You didn't stop or tell anybody?" asked Thomas.

Pru shook her head. She saw everybody's faces. "What is it? Why are you all staring at me?"

"The thing is, Pru," said Thomas, and his face was troubled, "just seconds before you tore in through the door of Campion's, Madame de Valentina claimed that she had made contact with your mother's spirit in the other world."

Rose thought that Pru, whose eyes had grown wide, would be indignant, but her reaction was quite different. Suddenly the tears stopped, and she smiled and cried, "So it's true! It's true. Madame de Valentina really can speak to the dead – and the dead can speak to us."

"Well, hang on..." said Rose, but Thomas shot her a warning look. Rose frowned. Thomas couldn't possibly believe. He was far too rational and thoughtful for that. When Rose had claimed to see Grace's dead husband Ned in the gallery while she was on stage at Campion's, Thomas had gently suggested that she was being fanciful. Surely he would think that Madame de Valentina was being just as fanciful when she said she had a message from Maud, or that she was having a chat with Pru's mother? But rather than upsetting Pru, this news seemed to have cheered her up enormously.

"There was something else," said Aurora. "Madame de Valentina said that your mother had left something for you." Pru frowned. "She said it was in the secret place that only you and she knew about."

"Do you know what she meant by that?" asked Thomas.

Pru scrambled to her feet.

"We haven't used it for years. I'd forgotten all about it. When I was little, Mama sometimes left me little treats. A sweetmeat, or a drawing, or a note in Italian – she never learned to read and write English with any fluency – if she knew I was coming back to the house alone. Often both she and my father would be out at work, and it was her way of letting me know she was thinking of me."

She was already by the fire, reaching up into the chimney breast and pulling away a loose brick. She gave a yelp and turned around, triumphant, holding up a St Christopher on a slender silver chain.

"My mama! My mama left me this!" There was

a ripple of astonishment around the room. Rose looked at the St Christopher. She recognised it. Mrs Smith had been wearing the St Christopher and chain when she and Effie had been at the house a little earlier. Why on earth would she remove it and put it in the secret place for Prudence to find? But Prudence was thrilled by her find.

"It's a miracle! A sign from my mama," she cried. "Madame de Valentina can talk with the dead. I must speak to her at once, so she can summon her spirit and I can say a proper goodbye to my dear mama."

10

Rose, Aurora, and Effie hurried through the streets towards the address that Thomas had given them. It was the lodging house where Madame de Valentina was staying. The fog lingered in patches, at times so thick it felt like breathing cotton wool. It was starting to snow lightly – the kind of snow that feels like icy midges swirling around your face. Although Thomas had pointed out that it was late, and Madame de Valentina was sure to be asleep in bed, Pru had become so agitated in her insistence that she had to see Elenora immediately that the girls had offered to go and ask if she would come.

"I bet she won't though," said Rose, as they walked quickly back towards St Olave's and

London Bridge, all holding hands to ensure they would not become separated in the thick fog that filled the streets by the river. "Because it will show her up as a charlatan. She won't be able to reproduce her trickery in Lant Street as easily as she can on the Campion's stage."

"But you can't be sure it's trickery," said Aurora. "How do you explain that she knew about Mrs Smith's death? Nobody had any idea that Mrs Smith was going to die. She was in fine fettle when you and Effie saw her just a few hours earlier."

"If anything, it makes it more astounding," said Effie. "If it was well known that Mrs Smith was ill, it might have been a lucky guess. But everyone knew she had made another recovery."

"There is something that's odd about it though," said Rose. "Mrs Smith was wearing the St Christopher this afternoon. I saw it. So why would she take it off and put it in the secret hiding place in the chimney, and leave it there for Pru? Did she know that she was going to die? And why leave it in the secret hiding place when Pru would find it anyway around her mother's neck?"

"Maybe she had a premonition of death," said Aurora.

"Or maybe Rose is right," said Effie. "The St Christopher itself isn't so important. It's the message it sends that is important. It provides evidence that Madame de Valentina really is in communication with the spirit world. Only Pru and her mama knew about the secret hiding place, so it suggests that the message really does come from beyond the grave."

"Exactly," said Rose. "The only thing the St Christopher really serves to prove is that Madame de Valentina is not a charlatan. It makes it appear that her mind really does rule the world, and that's a pretty powerful message to send out. People would queue up to be able to hear from their loved ones who had died, and it would guarantee a spot at the top of the bill at Campion's for weeks to come."

"Well, you can think what you like, Rosie," said Effie stoutly. "I find it comforting to think that she can bring me a message from my mother."

"But, Effie," said Rosie, "what did she actually tell you? She told you that your mum loved you. But you knew that already."

"She knew my mum's name was Iris."

"That wouldn't have been hard to find out. She could have asked around at Campion's. She could have gone to St Olave's churchyard and looked at the gravestone. Everyone at Campion's knows that's where she's buried. Most of them came to the funeral."

"What about the other things she got right?" said Aurora. "Judging by Thomas's face she hit the nail there. I didn't know he wasn't there when Maud and the twins died. And what about that family who had lost someone called Jack?"

"I don't know how to explain everything, but I bet I can explain how she knew about Jack. I'll show you after we've been to her lodgings."

"But even if you can explain that, it doesn't begin to explain how she knew that Pru's mum was dead," insisted Aurora.

"Or maybe," said Rose gravely, "she didn't know that Pru's ma was dead, but she knew that she was *about* to die."

"What do you mean?" demanded Effie. "Are you suggesting that Mrs Smith was murdered?"

"Oh, Rose, that's being awfully melodramatic," said Aurora quite crossly. "It's ridiculous. Madame de Valentina would hardly have time to leap off stage, rush to Lant Street, kill Pru's mum and run back, all without us noticing her absence."

"That's true," said Rose. "Maybe I'm being fanciful. But something doesn't feel right about it. First poor Ivy was murdered for no discernibly good reason, apart from the fact that she had made herself unpopular, and now somebody else connected with Campion's has died in mysterious circumstances."

"But there's no connection between the two deaths," said Effie. "And Dr Neagle said he wasn't surprised by Mrs Smith's death. He didn't think it was mysterious at all. He said that her heart could have given out at any time, and it was just ill-luck she fell face down on the cushion. I hate to say this, Rose, but you're jumping to conclusions. You took against Madame de Valentina before she even stepped on stage. Backstage this afternoon she was very nice, none of that prima donna behaviour you sometimes get with top-of-the-bill artistes. She was chatting to everyone."

Rose wondered if perhaps there was some truth in the accusation. Instinct told her there was something odd going on, but could she prove it – particularly when everyone else at Campion's seemed so gullible about Madame de Valentina's abilities? Now she came to think about it, Rose realised that the majority of Madame de Valentina's supposed messages from beyond the grave were for people with a connection with Campion's. Was it a way of getting them onside?

They had arrived at the address that Thomas had given them. The house was shrouded in darkness and turned in on itself, as if unwilling to yield up its secrets. It seemed surprisingly grimy to be the lodging of the glamorous Madame de Valentina. One small candle was just visible in a top window, which gave Rose the confidence to knock. A few seconds later they heard the sound of footsteps, and a man opened the door cautiously. He brandished a poker, but lowered it when he saw the girls.

"What do you want at this time of night?"

"We're sorry to disturb you. We know it's late but it's urgent. We wanted to speak to Madame de Valentina. She is lodging here."

The man snorted with laughter. "Well, I don't know about any Madame, but you can speak to Miss Elenora Valentina. She's not long back from that music hall. I told her we are respectable folk here, and she could have the top front room as long as she didn't bring any of that music-hall riff-raff here."

Rose lowered her head to avoid looking at Aurora and Effie, who she could see were trying not to laugh at being branded "music-hall riff-raff".

"We're nothing to do with the music hall," lied Rose smoothly. "We're here with a message."

"Well, you seem like nice girls, and Miss Valentina is respectable. Paid a month's rent in advance, so I can't complain."

"We would be so grateful if we could just see Miss Valentina for a brief moment," said Aurora, and her accent was so cut-glass that Rose wondered if that was how she sounded in the drawing room at Silver Square. It clearly impressed the man, who held open the door, pointed up the stairs and said, "Door at the top of the stairs."

They trooped up the stairs and Rose knocked.

"Madame de Valentina, can we come in?"

"Who is it?" The voice was gruff, with a hint of anxiety.

"It's Rose Campion, Thomas's daughter. I'm

here with my friends Aurora and Effie from the hall. We need to speak with you," said Rose keeping her voice low and hoping the landlord wasn't listening at the bottom of the stairs.

"I've retired to bed," came the reply.

"We've come from Prudence Smith," persisted Rose. "She is, as you can imagine, quite devastated by the death of her mother. She believes that you are a direct conduit between the living and the dead and she begged us to get you to come to Lant Street and contact her mother's spirit."

"You must send my apologies," came the voice. "I'm truly sorry, but I can't. I really can't." The voice quavered. "Tell Prudence how very sorry I am for her loss. But I can do nothing now for her."

Rose thought of the grief-stricken Prudence and she felt anger bubbling up inside her.

"So this is your mind that rules the world? Have a little decency. Prudence is distraught. The least you could do is come with us and visit her."

"I am sorry, but I simply cannot. Not now," said the voice firmly.

"Come on," said Rose to the others. "Let's

go. We're wasting our time here. There's just one thing I'd like to know, Miss Valentina. Your landlord told us that you had paid a month's rent in advance. But I know that Thomas had only booked you for one night. You must have been very confident that you would be staying on top of the bill to have paid a month's rent up front. Maybe you can't just commune with the dead and hypnotise people. Maybe you can predict the future too. Maybe you know when people are going to drop down dead."

Rose turned on her heel and marched down the stairs. The others looked at each other and followed. They let themselves out into the freezing night air.

"Well," said Aurora sarcastically, "that went well, Rose. You practically accused her of murdering Mrs Smith, which we've all agreed is impossible. She's going to be furious."

Thomas would be too, thought Rose, when he finds out what I said. She wondered whether Madame might pack up and depart, leaving Thomas with neither of his stars on the bill.

"She did seem genuinely upset by Mrs Smith's death," said Effie thoughtfully. "But Rose is right. There is something odd about her paying a month's rent in advance. As if she knew that her performance would be so show-stopping that Thomas would rush to engage her for much longer. Appearing to talk to a dead woman who nobody knew was dead was certainly fortuitous for Madame de Valentina. It's going to take quite some act to knock her off the top of the bill."

Rose was stomping along so fast that she occasionally disappeared completely into the fog. The others ran to catch up with her. On a night like tonight, the patches of fog were like shrouds. Someone could vanish into them.

"Where are you taking us?" demanded Effie. "We need to go back to Lant Street."

"We will, but we're going to make a quick detour via the graveyard," said Rose, turning the corner and holding open the iron gate of St Olave's churchyard for the others to pass through. It swung closed with a clang that echoed around the graveyard with a terrifying finality. They caught a glimpse of tiger tail streaking through the graveyard and disappearing into one of the many cracked and crumbling mausoleums – the tiger cub and Ophelia were hunting for rats.

The wispy fog clung to the tombstones, giving

them a disconcertingly eerie appearance, as if spirits were trying to wrap themselves around the masonry. Some graves seemed to appear and disappear as the fog drifted across the graveyard. A stone angel suddenly looming out of the fog made Effie scream, and the shriek echoed around the graveyard. The tiger skittered across the graveyard again, taking refuge in another mausoleum.

"Look," whispered Rose, pointing at a temporary wooden cross, which would eventually be replaced by a permanent gravestone. On the mound of earth in front of the cross were several bouquets of flowers. Most of them still had their labels on, proclaiming love for the dear departed "Daniel".

"What does that prove?" asked Aurora.

"Think back to Madame de Valentina's act, when she was claiming to channel the dead. Who was the first dead person she claimed was talking to her?"

"Jack," said Aurora. "She had a message from Jack."

"No!" said Effie, "there was somebody else before. Daniel! She said she had a message from Daniel, and what happened?"

"Nobody in the audience responded," said Aurora.

"Precisely," said Rose. "So what did Madame de Valentina do?"

"She moved on quickly, and said she had made contact with Uncle Jack, who had a message for Marge, or maybe it was Maggie, and for Joey and Meggie," said Aurora.

"Exactly," said Rose triumphantly, and she beckoned to them, disappearing into a patch of freezing fog as she led them a few rows further away from the first grave, to another cross and mound of earth. The flowers were still very fresh, and while some of the messages written on them had faded in the snow, a couple were still legible, including one that read, "To Uncle Jack, may you rest in peace, from your niece M, and Meggie and Joey".

Aurora frowned.

"So, Rose, are you suggesting that all Madame de Valentina did was come down to the graveyard, read the messages left on the flowers on top of the recently dug graves and then guess that one of their family members might be at Campion's?"

"I'd almost be prepared to bet on it," said

Rose. "It would be easy enough research to do. The alternative is that she really was talking to the dead. Which do you think is more likely?" She pointed to the message on the flowers on Jack's grave. "The names Jack, Meggie and Joey are clearly stated. But the niece just put her initial, M. And Madame de Valentina was very certain about the names Jack, Meggie and Joey, but she got the name of the niece wrong a couple of times before she hit on the right name."

"That's true," said Effie excitedly. "But we don't remember her wrong guesses so clearly. It's the right guess that sticks in our mind and makes us think that she really is talking to the dead."

"So," said Aurora and her tone was one of disappointment, "Madame de Valentina can no more talk to the dead than you and I? But do you think she is a complete fake? Can she really read people's minds and hypnotise them? And how did she know about Col and Florrie getting engaged, and that Tanner Street boy filching a watch?" Rose frowned. "I don't know, but I suppose she could have people hanging around the area and reporting back information to her."

Rose peered through the fog. She had thought she had heard a sound, but perhaps it was just the tiger cub and Ophelia hunting.

"You mean like spies?" asked Effie.

"How would they know that the people they spotted doing something significant were going to be at the performance that night?" asked Aurora.

"I wish I knew," said Rose.

"Besides," added Aurora. "It must cost a bob or two to employ the informants. Do you really think someone would go to all that bother just to stay top of the bill at Campion's for a month?"

"Maybe," said Rose thoughtfully, "there is a bigger prize in sight."

"What?" exclaimed Rory and Effie together.

"I haven't a clue," said Rose. She glanced around again. She had a strong sense they were being watched. She suddenly felt Ophelia weaving between her legs, and she bent and picked the cat up and stroked her under the chin. Ophelia purred in delight. Rose looked up and there was the tiger cub, sitting quite still in the middle of the path, its eyes watchful. It had definitely grown, but it was still very much a cub. Very slowly, and still holding Ophelia, she advanced towards it, holding out her hand. The cub observed her in a guarded fashion. Rose moved slowly towards the cub. Tentatively she put her hand under its chin and tickled it. She rubbed harder and the big cat purred loudly. Then it rolled on to its back and let Rose tickle its tummy. It purred delightedly. Ophelia jumped out of Rose's arms and bumped her nose against her fingers, demanding to be tickled too.

Carefully, Rose went to pick up the tiger cub, still feeling as if somebody was watching. The animal was surprisingly heavy, but sat contentedly in Rose's arms. It wasn't far to Campion's – if she could just get the animal back there, it could be kept safe until the zoo picked it up in the morning. She nodded to the others. Effie picked up Ophelia.

Rose moved her head sharply. She could hear something. She raised her eyebrows questioningly, and Effie and Rory nodded. They had heard it too. The girls stood shivering in silence, watching the patches of frozen fog floating across the gravestones. Rose frowned. She could hear footsteps – the kind of footsteps made by people trying to move quietly. They seemed to be converging from all sides of the graveyard. Rose put a finger to her lips and beckoned the others into a neglected mausoleum. The tomb's rusting iron gate had long stood broken, and there was evidence on the floor – a cigar butt, paper torn into tiny pieces – that they were not the only people to have been here recently. They stood well back in the darkness. Aurora and Effie were holding hands, and Effie put her other hand on Rose's shoulder. Rose could feel her fingers trembling. They heard feet, several pairs on the gravel, just a short distance away at the entrance of the tomb. Whoever was there was making much less of an attempt to disguise their presence. There were sounds above them too, as if people had clambered on top of the mausoleum.

Rose realised she had made a mistake. They were cornered in the mausoleum, with no way out. The tiger cub was still in her arms, but it was struggling, clearly nervous about the approaching noise. A flaming torch suddenly flared at the entrance to the mausoleum. The cub leapt out of Rose's arms, and as it did so, more flaming torches revealed the red, sweaty faces of two of the Tanner Street brothers, and maybe half a dozen of their friends. A cry went up –

"Catch the cat! Kill the beast! Skin the tiger!"
– and as the cub streaked out of the entrance
it was enveloped in a hastily constructed net
made of rope that had been dropped from above
the tomb. The crowd, some brandishing clubs
and knives, cheered. Rose rushed out of the
mausoleum and John, the oldest of the Tanner
Street boys, caught her round the waist and
pinned her arms behind her back. He laughed,
his breath hot with onions and beer.

"Well, thank you, Rose Campion, for all your
help. We've tried and failed the last few nights
to catch the beast, and you have very kindly
delivered it straight into our hands."

The cub was snarling and squirming fruitlessly
in the net, unable to find a way out.

"You better come out, we know you're there,"
called John.

Aurora and Effie emerged hesitantly into the
semicircle of young men.

"Well, well, well," said the other Tanner Street
boy, Len, with a sneer. "What a pretty pair:
lady muck and the thief," he said, looking at
Aurora and Effie. Both girls blushed, but they
looked straight ahead, their heads held up high
and defiantly. Rose wanted to cheer them. The

men started to jostle the girls in an intimidating fashion. Still gripped hard by John, Rose struggled as furiously as the tiger and shouted, "Leave them alone! Let us and the tiger go."

"Leave them alone! Let us go!" said the Tanner Street boy in a jeering, squeaky voice. Out of the corner of her eye, Rose could see that the tiger cub was making some progress in gnawing on the thin rope that had been used to make the improvised net. The Tanner Street boys had never been known for being good with their hands, except when it came to picking pockets.

"Shall we do what stuck-up Rose Campion asks, or shall we make her ask again?" said John. There was rowdy laughter and jeering. He poked her in the ribs. "Say please. Say pretty please."

Rose took a deep breath. The tiger cub was gnawing steadily. She needed to buy it time.

"Please let us go, and please don't hurt the tiger cub."

"Oh, we're going to let you all go. But first I'm going to make you watch what we're going to do to that tiger. That big moggie is going to be our payday. Tiger skins are worth a pretty penny."

"But that's such an ugly thing to do – and the

tiger is so beautiful!" said Aurora.

"It's all right for you," called a voice at the back of the crowd. "You've got pots of money, Lady Muck. But what about us? I've got mouths to feed. My share from the skin will buy shoes for my children."

The tiger had successfully gnawed through several bits of rope. The men seemed oblivious. Their focus was on the girls. Rose needed to play for more time. One man was sharpening his knife against another blade, as if preparing for the moment when he could stick it into the cub. It was a sickening sound.

Something that the man had said about buying shoes for his children gave Rose a stab of hope. Maybe she could get them all out of this situation. But it was a risky strategy.

"So when you sell the tiger skin, are you all getting equal shares?" she asked, hoping against hope that she knew the double-dealing Tanner Street boys as well as she thought she did.

"Of course we are," said one of the youths. "It's all agreed. A guinea each for being part of the tiger hunt."

"Yes," said another man with a deep scar on his cheek. "Equal shares all round."

"Oh," said Rose innocently, "so if you are only getting a guinea each, who's getting the rest?"

Some of the men looked at her with interest, and one muttered, "What do you mean, the rest?"

She could see Len looked shifty, and John, who was holding on to her, shifted uncomfortably and loosened his grip, which made her think she was on the right track.

"Here, hop it, all of you," he said to the girls. "Run before I change my mind. We've got men's work to do." He turned to his chums. "Let's get to work on the beast."

"Wait, I want to hear what Rose Campion has to say," said the scarred man. "I want to know how much a tiger skin is actually worth. And if we're being cheated by those Tanner Street scum…"

John took a swing at the man, who hit him back. A brawl broke out, and as it did, the tiger tried to scramble out of the hole it had gnawed in the net. One of its hind legs got caught, but Rose bent to untangle it, whispered "Run!" and watched as it streaked across the graveyard and over the wall, unnoticed by the fighting men.

Rose, Effie and Aurora took flight too, eager to

be away before the men realised that they had lost their prize. They were halfway down the lane and beyond reach before the men realised that not just the girls, but also the tiger, had got clean away.

The Tanner Street boy's threatening voice carried across the frozen air.

"I'll get you back for this, Rose Campion. You see if I don't."

The girls ran all the way to Lant Street, only stopping when they got to Pru's door, where they fell into a breathless, trembling huddle that was laced with terror and relief.

"Rosie," asked Aurora after a moment. "How much *is* a tiger skin worth?"

Rose shrugged. "I have absolutely no idea. I was just certain that the Tanner Street boys wouldn't pass up the opportunity to swindle the others if they could, so I took the chance."

She saw their horrified faces. Aurora shook her head incredulously.

"One day you are going to come a cropper, Rosie Campion. But I don't mind admitting that if it wasn't for your quick thinking, that poor tiger would be dead."

11

It was a sad party that made its way back to Campion's in the early hours of the morning, where Grace and Perdita put poor Pru to bed and made her take the sleeping draught that Dr Neagle had prepared for her. Pru had been distraught when Rose told her that Madame de Valentina refused to come. Thomas had soothed the situation, saying that he would try to persuade Madame de Valentina to give Pru a private reading very soon, but Rose wasn't convinced he was doing the right thing. Surely by encouraging Pru he was suggesting there was some truth in Madame's claim to be conversing with the spirit world. He couldn't possibly believe it, could he? He must know it was all just an act, and Madame de Valentina was faking it. But she recalled Thomas's face when Elenora claimed to be bringing him a message from Maud and the twins. His features had been wreathed with love and pain – but also with hope too. People wanted to believe that death wasn't final, and that one day they would be reunited with their loved ones.

On the journey back to Campion's, Rose, Aurora and Effie had told the others what had happened to them with the Tanner Street boys in the graveyard. Thomas was furious.

"They're banned," he said. "I won't have them in the place with their threats and violence."

Rose frowned. She was worried banning them would only rile them more. But Thomas had made up his mind and wouldn't budge.

Lottie had been waiting up for them when they got back to Campion's. She collared Rose.

"That woman you employed for the evening, Ella, is still in the kitchen. I offered to pay her off so she could go, but she was quite insistent about waiting for you, Rosie. I thought you might want to keep her on. Cook said she's a grafter. Hope I did the right thing."

"Of course you did, Lottie."

Rose pushed open the door of the kitchen,

expecting to find Ella asleep in a chair by the range, but she was sweeping the floor. Rose's eyes opened wider. Every surface in the kitchen was gleaming. Even the wall above the range, which had been covered in soot for months, had been scrubbed. Ella had her back to Rose and as she swept she hummed a tune that Rose recognised as an old music-hall ballad. She turned when she heard Rose, and Rose saw that her eyes were moist.

Rose took the broom out of her hand and said gently, "Sit down and rest. You must be exhausted. I paid you to clean the pots, not scrub the entire kitchen. You've quite transformed the place. I hardly recognise it."

"I always knew my talent for housework would be useful one day," said Ella with a wry smile.

"Would you like to stay on?" asked Rose. "We could do with another pair of hands in the kitchen. If you're going to work as hard as you have tonight, we can pay you more too."

Ella hesitated. "I don't want more money, but I do need somewhere to stay. At least temporarily, until I can get back on my feet. I had some bad luck. I have nothing to my name but the clothes I'm wearing."

Rose nodded, and could see from Ella's face that she shouldn't question the woman further.

"Of course you can stay. We don't have a spare room, but you can use one of the mattresses from the props cupboard in here for as long as you need."

Ella smiled, and despite her matted hair, grey skin and the dark circles under her eyes, she suddenly looked radiant, and at least fifteen years younger.

"Would you mind if I boiled up water in the copper for a wash? I would love to have clean hair again."

"You'd be very welcome," said Rose.

Ella followed Rose to the prop's cupboard to get the mattress.

"I hear Madame de Valentina made quite a stir tonight," said Ella as they carried the mattress back to the kitchen.

"You could say that," said Rose. "She's staying on, top of the bill for weeks, I imagine. We'll add the pantomime to the bill when we've rehearsed it, and that will bring in the crowds. Madame will perform alternate late and early shows. You should pop out one evening during her act to watch."

"I'd like that," said Ella lightly. "I'm very curious to see her."

"You won't be the only one. We're going to be packed out with people wanting her to contact the dead for them."

"Do you think she really is talking to the dead?" asked Ella.

Rose shook her head vigorously.

"No, not for a moment. It's an act – a clever act, but still an act. People believe what they want to believe. Perhaps whatever they need to make life bearable. I think she's a charlatan, preying on people's misery. What about you? Do you think it's possible that she really is speaking with the dead?"

"No," said Ella. "I haven't glimpsed her yet, but I am completely confident that Madame de Valentina is a fraud in every way."

* ✳ *

The following afternoon, Rose, Effie, Aurora, Grace and Perdita gathered in Thomas's study. Thomas, thought Rose tenderly, looked tired and a little fragile, as if he was recovering from an illness or a shock. They were waiting for Edward when Effie picked up the folded morning newspaper on Thomas's desk, untouched even though it was almost three o' clock.

"Look at this!" said Effie, pointing to the headline. "Lord and Lady Fitzcillian lose priceless heirloom in mystery robbery." She turned to Aurora and Grace. "You know these people, don't you, Rory?"

Aurora picked up the paper and scanned it. "I do. Look," she said to Grace and Perdita, pointing to the story. "We were only at their house for tea a few days ago." She skimmed through the report. "It says the stolen item was a diamond brooch, presented to the family by Charles II. But there was no sign of a break-in and all of the outer doors were locked, so the police are treating it as an inside job."

Perdita frowned.

"Lady Fitzcillian showed us that brooch," said Grace excitedly. "She was very proud of it."

"I remember," said Rory. "And very ugly it was too. Not like the Easingford Emeralds. I can't imagine why anyone would want to steal it."

Perdita gave a sharp laugh. "I very much doubt that whoever took it was planning to wear it. They will sell it, no doubt for a pretty penny, once the hue and cry dies down."

Edward arrived and they showed him the paper, before Thomas called them all to order.

"I wanted to get your advice, all of you. I'm not happy at the prospect, but I want you all to know that I'm seriously thinking about cancelling the pantomime this year."

There were cries of protest from the girls, and even Edward shook his head and said, "Oh, Thomas!"

Thomas gave a rueful shrug.

"In my heart I knew that would be your reaction. But I'm not sure how we will manage. We've already announced it's *Cinderella*, so we can't change the title. But the casting is impossible. We lost our Cinderella when Ivy died, and I still haven't found a replacement. And now we've lost our Prince Charming, at least until Pru feels ready to return. The last thing she said before she went off with her aunt and uncle is that she wouldn't be back until after Christmas. With all the difficulties, I wonder whether it's better to cancel the pantomime altogether, and just run the normal programme with Madame de Valentina top of the bill until Christmas and beyond, if she's still pulling the crowds."

"But the panto is a Campion's tradition," said Rose. "We're one of the few small halls to do one. If we don't do it, the people of Southwark and Bermondsey will be so disappointed. They look forward to it."

"I'm well aware of that," sighed Thomas. "But there are so many obstacles this year. I've only got one Ugly Sister, although I could get Lottie to fill in, but I never quite trust what the chorus will do when she isn't there to keep them in check. Last time she was off, all the ballet girls stuck out their tongues at the audience at the end of the dying swan routine. Oh, and I thought I had Bullingdon Bertie lined up for the dame – but he's been arrested for larceny and is going to be in prison this Christmas, not pantoland."

"Well," said Edward, "if you really don't want to do the panto this year, Thomas, we will all respect your decision. But if it helps, I could play the dame for you."

There was a scream of delight from Effie. Thomas looked taken aback. So did Perdita. Aurora's eyes widened, and she glanced at Grace from under her eyelashes.

"Edward, dear boy, there is a world of

difference between playing Hamlet in the West End and playing the pantomime dame on the Campion's stage," said Thomas. "You may find that your high-society friends are shocked. I can guarantee that there will be gossip. Some will say that your reputation is ruined."

"I've no doubt you're right, Thomas," said Edward. "But a person's reputation is quite different from his character." Then he added with a wicked smile, "And just think what fun it would be. I've always wanted to play the dame. And if it means I'm invited to a dozen less soirées, I can't say I'll be sorry."

Aurora stood up, walked over to Rose, who was standing by the door, linked arms with her and said, "If you are playing the dame, Edward, then I'm going to be an Ugly Sister with Rose."

For a moment Edward looked troubled. "Look here, Rory," he said. "I'm a grown-up and I can decide that I don't give a jot for my reputation. But it's different for you. Some people would think it scandalous, and if your reputation is ruined it will affect your entire future. Every drawing-room door in the country will be closed to you. You may say that you don't care now, but you might feel differently in the future."

"Oh, Edward," said Aurora. "Just a few months ago I had never seen the inside of a drawing room, and honestly from what I've seen of them so far I wouldn't mind if I never stepped inside another one."

Rose gave a little inward cheer.

"But," said Aurora, "although I don't mind for myself, what about you, Grace? Would it make you too uncomfortable if your niece and chief bridesmaid were performing in the Campion's pantomime? Would Sir Godfrey be so scandalised that he would break off your engagement?"

Grace hesitated, but before she could speak, Rose, unable to contain her excitement, cut over her.

"But why would Sir Godfrey ever have to know that Aurora is appearing in the Campion's panto? She will be completely unrecognisable under her wig and costume. She can play under an assumed name, not as Miss Aurora Easingford. Only the sharpest-eyed regular would ever have the faintest suspicion it was you."

"That's true!" said Effie. "It's so simple and brilliant."

Aurora looked at her father and he nodded his approval, and then she looked at Grace.

"I'd love to do it. Edward is right – it would be such fun. But if you don't want me to, Grace, I will completely understand."

Grace's face was serious. For a moment, Rose thought she was going to say that she was uncomfortable with the idea. But then a great beam spread across her features.

"Of course you must do it, Rory. And if you can play an Ugly Sister under an assumed name, then I can play Prince Charming under an alias too. At least up until the wedding on Boxing Day. Pru can take over after that."

"Grace!" said Edward worriedly. "Are you sure? If Sir Godfrey finds his future wife parading across the Campion's stage he might not be best pleased." Rose thought that was an understatement: she thought that Grace's kind but stuffy fiancé would be outraged.

"He need never know. Just as long as nobody at Campion's tells him, he will be none the wiser. I'll be performing under an assumed name too, and I'll be unrecognisable dressed up as a boy."

Thomas frowned. "Are you quite sure that you want to do this, Grace? It's risky."

"It is," said Grace. "But Edward is right – it will be fun, and it feels like a long time since I had any real fun." She looked sad. "Why not have one last hurrah."

Thomas looked around the room. "So are we all agreed?"

"Oh no we're not," shouted Effie with a grin.

"Oh yes we are," shouted everyone else.

"Wonderful," said Thomas. "Then you shall all go to the ball. All I have to do now is find a Cinderella."

"What about you, Perdita?" asked Rose.

"What, me? On stage!?"

"Why not?" said Grace. "I've seen you acting with Freddie, and you really are very talented. And you clearly love it."

Perdita shook her head. "I can't. I'm sorry. I would love to play Cinderella, but I can't act on stage." She bit her lip, and, as if giving herself a little pep talk, she muttered under her breath, "You mustn't. You made a promise."

Everyone looked at Perdita curiously. She always seemed so calm and collected.

"No matter," said Thomas heartily. "There will be someone at Campion's whose foot fits the glass slipper."

12

The parlour at Lant Street was almost in darkness. A small candle guttered in the draught from the ill-fitting windows. A wind had whipped up and the windows were rattling. There was a distant sound of thunder. Everyone was gathered around a table that had been placed in the centre of the room. Rose shivered. She didn't want to be here, but it would have looked churlish to refuse to come after Madame de Valentina had sent a note to Thomas, saying that although she was always happy to give private hypnosis demonstrations, she didn't normally give what she called "private readings". Nonetheless, for Prudence and "a small group of friends from Campion's" she would make a rare exception because of the tragic circumstances surrounding

Pru's mother's death. Effie mused that maybe Rose's outburst at the lodging house had contributed to this decision.

Thomas had suggested that the attempt to contact Pru's mother took place in Campion's after that evening's performance, but Madame de Valentina had insisted it take place in Lant Street, on the grounds that she would "be closer to Mrs Smith's spirit there". Pru and her uncle and aunt had been banished from the Lant Street parlour by Madame de Valentina since darkness had fallen, and had taken refuge at Campion's. Rose raised an eyebrow when Pru told her that Elenora had said she needed time alone in the house to prepare. She suspected it was just a ruse so that she could stage-manage her trickery, but Pru was convinced of Madame de Valentina's honesty.

"Mama and I didn't get a chance to say goodbye. I never got a chance to tell her how much I loved her. If I could only speak to her one last time I would be content."

"We will begin," said Elenora de Valentina to the assembled company, which included everyone except Perdita, who had cried off, saying she was going to visit a friend in Herne

Bay and would be away overnight.

Madame de Valentina went around the room, blowing out every candle except for a small one illuminating her place at the table. The air was heavy with the scent of lilies from a large bouquet that Sir Godfrey had sent to Pru, expressing his sorrow at her mother's death. In front of Madame de Valentina were several sheets of paper and a pen, which she had explained were for "automatic writing", which occurred when a spirit from the dead took control of her hands and mind and dictated her a message.

"We will all hold hands," breathed Elenora in a husky voice.

The candle in front of her gutted. A flash of lightning was suddenly visible through a tiny crack in the drawn parlour curtains, followed by another roll of thunder. Rose tried to peer around the room, but she couldn't make out anyone in the gloom. All she could feel were the warm fingers of Effie and Rory, clutching each of her hands. The candlelight caught Elenora's face for a moment and Rose frowned: she knew she had seen that face before somewhere.

There was a sudden gust of freezing air in the room.

"The spirits are with us," said Madame de Valentina in mournful tones. "Can you hear me?"

There was another gust of icy wind and a sharp rap on the table that made everyone jump and Effie scream.

"Is that Mrs Smith?" asked Elenora.

There was a flurry of angry raps on the table, and it tilted so violently that everyone broke hands to try and steady it. Who was making it move? Rose tried to peer under the tablecloth, but it was made of heavy damask and reached right to the floor. It must be a trick. Somebody must be under the table, thought Rose. She raised her foot and waved it around underneath the table, but encountered nothing but thin air.

"I'm hearing a voice," said Elenora Valentina. "It's very faint." She closed her eyes and put her hands to each side of her temple, concentrating with her forehead furrowed.

"Is it my mama?" cried Pru, but Elenora raised a warning hand to silence her.

"No, it's a man. His name is Ed, or maybe it's Ned. He's asking for Grace."

"Ned! Yes, yes, I'm here," squeaked Grace.

"Ned wants you to know that he is delighted

by your decision, and he thinks you are being brave. He will always be watching over you and little Freddie. He says there is no need for you to worry. Freddie will be much happier very, very soon."

"Oh, thank you, thank you," cried Grace and everyone could hear the tears in her voice.

Rose frowned in the darkness. It was all so vague. What decision was being referred to? Grace's determination to appear in the pantomime? But that was a secret. Her decision to accept Sir Godfrey's proposal? Or did it refer to Grace's decision to wear her red frock today, rather than her blue one? It was preposterous. You could interpret it in any way that pleased you. Or, supposed Rose, the way that most comforted you.

Rose frowned again. Grace hadn't said anything about Freddie being unhappy. Rose had had a horrible time when Thomas had got it into his head to send her to Miss Pecksniff's Academy for Young Ladies for a year. All the other girls had looked down on her for not being a proper lady. Rose wondered whether Freddie was at the receiving end of similar bullying at his school. She hoped not.

There was another gust of cold air, followed by a flash of lightning and a clap of thunder, so loud that it felt as if the small house was quaking. Maybe Madame de Valentina's apparently wondrous mind extended to controlling the weather?

Madame de Valentina appeared to be in some kind of trance. She jerked forward like a doll, and then said in a strange voice, "It's Ivy. Tell Thomas that I'm top of the bill in the great music hall in the sky."

Rose suppressed a snort of laughter, turning it into a bout of coughing. She was terribly afraid she was going to get a fit of the giggles. Elenora was glaring in her direction.

"Prudencia! Prudencia! Your mother is here. Her voice is very faint. I can barely hear her. She wants me to write a message for you so that you will have a memento from her that you can treasure forever. She will deliver the message in her own words, guiding my hand over the paper."

"Please do!" cried Pru. "Oh, Mama!" She burst into tears.

Elenora was writing furiously, her hand crossing the paper faster than an express train.

The page was illuminated by the candle and, leaning over to get a better look, Rose saw that the writing was a distinctive, neat copperplate. Madame's eyes were glazed, as if she was lost in another world, but her hand continued to write. She had covered several pages. Finally, she put down the pen and leaned back in her chair. Her pale face was glistening with sweat, and she momentarily shut her eyes as if exhausted. She took a deep breath and opened them again, and then she handed the paper and the candle to Pru, who held the flame close to the paper and read out loud. There was wonder in her voice and tears poured down her cheeks.

The contents, Rose thought, were not particularly memorable. There was a reverie about a week that Pru and her mother had spent in Broadstairs, and some housekeeping advice and plenty of expressions of love, as well as comforting words about her death: instantly, apparently, as the result of a heart attack, as Dr Neagle had surmised. Rose rather hoped that if she were ever to receive a message from beyond the dead, it would be something more spectacular than nostalgia about a trip to the seaside and exhortations to wear a front-door key on a chain about her neck at all times, and not to neglect to wear her vest.

But Pru seemed quite delighted with her message. When she stopped reading, she raised her head to Madame de Valentina, her eyes shining as she thanked her.

"Mama says that she can rest in peace on the other side, now that she has communicated with me."

Madame de Valentina gave a tight smile. "Yes, she can. I sense that she is already far away now. You must let her sleep the sleep of eternity, Pru. There will be no more contacting her."

Pru became weepy again. "You mean I will not be able to speak to Mama again?"

"It is most unlikely," said Elenora, and her voice was kind. Then she added firmly, "She harnessed my powers to communicate her final goodbye in the letter. You must let her rest."

"I will treasure it forever," said Pru, holding the letter against her heart.

"Can I see the letter, Pru?" asked Rose gently.

Pru reverently handed it to Rose, who tipped the candle closer so that she could read it. Her eyes skimmed several lines, confirming what she had suspected. For a moment Rose hesitated, aware that what she was about to do might be construed as a kind of cruelty. But was it such cruelty to expose a charlatan?

"Pru," she said, "am I right in thinking that you and your mother spoke to each other mostly in Italian?"

Pru nodded. Even in the gloom, Rose could see Elenora's eyes glinting and boring into her. The silence in the room felt thick and sticky.

"And am I also right that your mama could barely read and write English?"

Again, Pru nodded.

"So," said Rose quietly, "don't you think it odd that this letter, which Madame de Valentina claims is written entirely in your mother's words, is also written in perfect English?"

There was a buzz around the room, and a sharp intake of breath from Thomas.

Pru burst into violent tears, and Rose felt as if she was the scoundrel, just for pointing out what to her was obvious. They were all being willingly fooled by Madame de Valentina, just as an audience allows itself to be willingly fooled by a stage magician. Elenora fixed her gaze on Rose with such intensity that Rose felt like prey, about to be swallowed by a predator.

"The dead work in mysterious ways," Elenora said, in a calm voice as smooth as velvet. "Pru, you must of course make up your own mind. It is entirely up to you if you wish to put your faith in the possibility that your mother lives on in the world beyond, and that the two of you will eventually be reunited. But, of course, if you choose to deny your mother, and spurn the words that she has offered up as a gift to you that is entirely your choosing."

As if in answer, Pru grabbed the letter that now lay on the table and held it to her breast. Thomas caught Rose's eye as if warning her that now was not the time and place to say more, so Rose kept quiet. No recently bereaved daughter, she realised, whose grief was still as raw and open as a wound, was going to deny her own mother. Rose looked around the serious faces, illuminated only by the single flickering candle at the table, and thought how spectral they all looked. Thomas was right. This was not the time or place to argue about Madame de Valentina's sincerity or falsity. Everyone was still too shell-shocked by the deaths so close to home. But she could no longer subscribe to this charade. She stood up to leave, but as she did so, another gust of cold air whirled through the room.

"Hold hands, we must not break the circle," urged Madame de Valentina. "We have another spirit trying to make contact. We will lose the spirit if we are not quick."

"My mama," cried Pru, and there was such anguish in her pleading eyes that Rose reluctantly sat down again and joined hands. The room was suddenly lit up by a flash of lightning that briefly illuminated everyone's faces, looking scared and white, followed by a low rumble of thunder. Without warning, the table suddenly tilted again, appearing to rise up and down as precariously as a ship tossed upon a stormy sea. Madame de Valentina grabbed the candle and the party broke hands, and once again started to try and steady the table.

"We have a very restless spirit in the room," said de Valentina. "I must help it. Who's there?" she asked gently.

The table tipped again, and a draught of icy air filled the room. The lone candle was suddenly snuffed out and fell to the floor with a clatter. Someone screamed, and Rose could hear Effie's frightened breathing beside her.

"I have a message for someone here," said

a voice. It was coming from the direction of Madame de Valentina, but it didn't sound anything like her. The voice sounded very wispy and far away.

"Who is the message for?" asked Elenora, sounding much more like her normal self.

"It is for Rose."

"For me?" squeaked Rose uncertainly. "Who is it?"

"It's me, your mother." Rose gave a cry like a wounded animal and there were gasps of astonishment from the others. Rose felt faint. She had always longed to find and speak to her mother, but not like this. She had pictured the two of them sitting together somewhere cosy, and imagined the conversations they might have together – exchanges full of wonder, as they told each other of their separate lives since the moment when Rose had been stolen from her pram. She had spent years scanning the faces of women she saw in the street, wondering if they would perhaps be her lost mother. She was well aware that it was possible that her mother was long dead, but in her heart she had carried the hope that she was out there somewhere, and that one day they would find each other. And for everything she had just said and thought about Elenora de Valentina being a fraud, she still felt as if all her hopes had been cruelly snuffed out.

"Tell me your name?" stuttered Rose, her throat feeling as if it was closing over.

"My darling Rose, my name is Nell." The voice was very faint.

"When did you die? Where? Where are you buried?"

"I cannot hear you, Rose. I am too far away, and the connection between my world and yours is like a broken bridge. But you must know that I never stopped looking for you until the day I died."

Rose made a choking noise. "How did you die? When?" she demanded.

"I love you, Rose," said the voice. "I will not come again. Remember me. Remember..." The words tailed off.

A mixture of astonishment, fury and misery swirled in Rose's head and heart. She felt as if she could barely breathe. With a cry she stood up, and blindly she made her way to the parlour door, pulled it open, and felt her way to the front door. Without stopping, she ran out into the street and set off in the direction of Campion's, hardly aware of where she was going. Behind her she could hear Thomas calling her name, his voice urgent and anxious, but she didn't stop. She ran, unseeingly, until she found herself alone in St Olave's graveyard. The storm had passed and there was only an odd rumble of thunder from far away.

She slumped down on one of the gravestones, oblivious to the damp stone beneath her. Conflicting emotions and confusion turned to hot tears. Either she was the victim of some kind of horrible trickery, or Madame de Valentina really had made contact with her mother, which could only mean that the woman who she had so longed to be reunited with was dead. The rational part of Rose was convinced it was all a ruse. But why would Madame de Valentina choose her? Maybe it was because Rose had made her scepticism about Madame's psychic powers so obvious?

On the other hand, now that she too had apparently received a message from beyond the grave, Rose could understand why those who did were so powerfully affected. She wanted to believe that her lost mother had spoken to her. But she was also devastated to discover that her mother was dead. She simply didn't know what to think. Tears fell down her face and she was suddenly aware of the tiger cub, sitting and watching her solemnly, its head turned to one side as if sympathising with her. Rose smiled at the cub and held out her hand, and it leapt on to her lap. Rose stayed stroking the cub for several minutes and it purred with evident pleasure. She wondered if the cub would let her carry it back to Campion's, but when she tried to stand up it bounded away and scrambled up the wall, where it sat watching her.

* ✻ *

Rose knew she had to go back to Campion's. It wasn't fair on Thomas, who would be anxious. It was starting to snow heavily. On a night like tonight, she didn't want the others out looking for her. Disconsolately she kicked a stone, and it shot across the path and hit a headstone with such force that the stone moved. Rose moved closer, feeling guilty that she had damaged the gravestone, which was now leaning drunkenly to one side, and was even more aghast to discover that it was Effie's mother's tombstone. Clearly it was in need of more permanent repair than that instigated by Sir Godfrey at Ivy's funeral. Perhaps some animal was burrowing there, because the gap under the stone had reappeared. She wedged it back in place as best she could and set off for Campion's.

The snow was coming down thickly now, as if the clouds above were trying to empty themselves as quickly as possible. It was eerily quiet, well after midnight, and everyone was in bed on a night like tonight. Rose walked as briskly as she dared, cutting down Bleeding Heart Alley to lessen the distance. She couldn't wait to be back in the warmth of Campion's, where she was certain that Thomas would be waiting for her. On a couple of occasions, she thought she heard footsteps following her, but when she turned there was nobody there, and by the third time she realised that what she was hearing was the echo of her own feet, crunching across the blanket of snow.

She slipped into Rat Trap Wynd, a narrow little winding alley, pleased that she was so close to home. She turned a corner and there, silhouetted at the far end of the alley, was a figure, standing still as a sentry. Rose recognised John, the eldest of the Tanner Street boys. Her heart began to hammer in her chest. She had a choice: she could turn and run, or she could saunter on boldly, as if she had no fear. Without missing a step, she settled on the latter course of action. A nasty smile crossed the young man's face.

"Well, if it isn't little Miss Rose Campion. Out all on her own at this time of night."

Rose went to push by him, but he grabbed her and pulled her a few feet further back into the alley. She could feel a knife blade tickling her throat. Rose felt sick and her legs and arms felt heavy. She knew that the Tanner Street boys were all bluff and bluster, but nonetheless she didn't like being at the mercy of one of them in the middle of the night. She thought it unlikely that John would cut her throat, but she wasn't entirely confident that he might not slash her face if riled. She could imagine him boasting to his friends for years to come that the scar on Rose Campion's cheek came from his knife.

"You got me and my brothers banned from that poxy music hall of yours," he hissed. "You're going to pay for that, Rose Campion." He traced the point of his knife over her cheek.

Rose felt frozen, as if all her strength and her wits had suddenly deserted her. She didn't dare speak, in case her voice came out in a squeak. Her only hope was that he was just toying with her, and that he would eventually get bored, particularly now that the snow was swirling around them, heavy and wet.

"Let me go, John," said Rose. "We can go back to Campion's and talk to Thomas. Maybe he'll change his mind about banning you."

The boy laughed, and it was not a pleasant sound. In one swift, sharp movement Rose elbowed him in the stomach. John loosened his grip and Rose was off, fast as lightning. But he was on her almost immediately, pushing her to the ground and bringing his entire weight down on her, so that she was pushed flat on her back. He tickled her neck with the point of his knife.

Suddenly Rose was aware of the crack of a pistol, and a bullet whizzed by the Tanner Street boy's cheek. There was another crack and a bullet sped by his head, so close it grazed the top of his hair. His ugly smile turned to terror.

"Let her go," came a clear voice. John needed no further exhortation. He scrambled to his feet, leaving Rose spread-eagled on the ground, and scarpered. Another two bullets whizzed past

Rose and helped John on his way.

Warily, Rose sat up. Perdita stood further down the alley. She was blowing nonchalantly on a small pistol. She took a few steps and offered Rose a hand, hauling her to her feet.

"Lucky I came along," she said in a light voice. "I'll walk with you back to Campion's just to make sure you're quite safe."

Rose had recovered her voice. "Thank you," she said. "I will be eternally grateful to you."

"Nasty pieces of work, those Tanner Street boys. I'm really rather sorry that I missed."

"You weren't actually trying to kill him, were you?" asked Rose, shocked.

"I'm joking," said Perdita lightly. "I wouldn't hurt a fly."

"Why do you keep a pistol in your bag?" asked Rose.

"Protection," said Perdita briskly. "If you were bought up in tiger country like I was, it didn't do to leave the house without one."

"But there are no tigers in London," said Rose, before realising her mistake. "Well, only one, anyway."

"Ah," said Perdita darkly, "but there are other predators in London. From what I've seen of it, it's a veritable jungle. It's always good to be prepared."

Rose frowned. "But what are you doing here? Aren't you supposed to be in Herne Bay?"

"Plans change," said Perdita shortly.

They arrived outside Campion's and Perdita turned.

"Aren't you coming in?" asked Rose.

"No," said Perdita. She hesitated. "Probably best not to mention the pistol, Rose. Not everyone would be as sanguine about it as you." She paused. "In fact, maybe just don't mention that you saw me at all. I would be grateful."

Rose nodded. She felt she was in Perdita's debt. She watched while Perdita walked briskly away. At the corner she turned and smiled.

"Keep safe, Rose. Stay out of harm's way. I can't bear the thought of any child being lost."

Then she was gone, disappearing into the falling snow like a ghost.

13

The pantomime was starting to come together. The morning had been spent rehearsing: Dolores had been reluctantly roped in to play Cinderella, and although she was not a natural actress, she had charm, and her popularity with the Campion's audience would see her through. But Rose still wondered how Perdita would have fared in the role, and what she had meant when she said that she had made a promise never to appear on stage again.

Rose and Rory loved working together again, their natural chemistry making Thomas hope that their double act as the Ugly Sisters might be a memorable comic turn. They had incorporated the bicycle into their performance, despite Thomas's initial concern that, to the Campion's crowd, the bicycle act was so associated with the pair that doing it might unwittingly reveal Aurora's true identity. But everyone else had said that he was being far too cautious.

"Once I'm in my costume even my own father won't recognise me," said Rory confidently.

The rehearsal had gone well, although Rose had been rather subdued and every now and again she had seen Thomas giving her a sideways look, as if checking up on her. When she had returned to Campion's the previous evening, Thomas had tried to talk to her about what had happened in Lant Street, but Rose had felt too drained after the evening's events, and her encounter with the Tanner Street boy, to respond.

She had gone to bed and lain awake into the early hours thinking about her narrow escape, pondering Perdita's unexpected appearance and, most of all, thinking about Elenora de Valentina's claim to have communicated with her dead mother.

But now work was stopping her from thinking too much about the revelation of the previous evening. And she didn't want to think about it. She didn't believe that Elenora could talk with the dead, so why did the information that her mother was dead hurt so much? She glanced around the room and her eye met Perdita's, who was sitting at a table in the middle of the auditorium reading the morning newspaper. Perdita gave a little conspiratorial wink. She didn't usually attend rehearsals and Rose wondered if she had come to check up on her. She was reading a newspaper whose headline screamed about last night's mysterious robbery at Lady Plockton's – a story that everyone had discussed excitedly when they had gathered first thing. The police were saying that, just as in the Fitzcillian robbery, there was no sign of a break-in, so they were treating it as another inside job.

* ✳ *

Ella was at the back of the auditorium, shining the great mirrors behind the mahogany bar. Every few minutes she would stop and gaze at what was happening on stage, as if transfixed, then return to her job with even more gusto. If she carried on working at this rate, Thomas was going to have to double her wages.

Ella worked her way up the auditorium towards the stage, polishing the mirrors and keeping one eye on the rehearsal. Rose had noticed that she often found a job to do in the auditorium when they were rehearsing. She wondered if she was a little stage-struck.

Ella had drawn level to where Perdita, who was still reading and oblivious to anyone else, was sitting. Rose saw Ella glance sideways at Perdita. She looked again more closely. A change came over her face, and Ella's mouth made a little mewl of surprise, before she recovered herself and turned sharply away and walked back towards the kitchen. Rose frowned. It was an odd, extreme reaction to the other woman. Did they know each other? Perdita had looked up at the sound and given no indication that she recognised Ella, barely giving the other woman a second glance. Rose resolved to ask Ella about it later when she got the chance.

"Rose! Rose! Wakey-wakey." She looked up. Thomas was asking her whether she had an opinion on the ballet sequence. Rose shook her head. She had barely been watching. Thomas let it go and they moved on to an aerial flying scene, which had been inserted into the story and which allowed Grace to show off some of her skills. Watching it, Rose thought how Grace seemed to come fully alive when performing – almost as if somebody had suddenly filled in her outline in vivid colours.

"I love this," she said, her eyes sparkling and shining as she was gently lowered to the ground. Rose and Rory helped her unbuckle her harness.

"It'll be better still when you are doing it in front of an audience," said Rose softly.

Grace nodded. "I know. I've had such fun these last few days of rehearsal. I know how addictive it can be in front of an audience. I'm worried that I'll get back my taste for it, and then I'll struggle to give it up again when I become Lady Caskins."

"Then maybe you shouldn't," said Rose lightly.

Rory nudged Rose in the ribs, and Grace raised an eyebrow.

"You mean I shouldn't marry Sir Godfrey, or shouldn't give up performing?" asked Grace.

"Both. Look, Grace, tell me to mind my own business, but you clearly love performing, so why give it up so easily?"

"Oh, Rose," said Grace. "It's not been an easy decision."

Rose looked around. Everybody else was busy. Thomas had moved on to rehearsing a scene with Edward.

"But why marry a man you obviously don't love?" said Rose fiercely.

"Rose!" said Aurora, shocked by her directness.

Grace sighed. "Rose is right. I don't love Godfrey – at least, not in the way I loved Ned. But maybe you only get one chance to love like that. Sir Godfrey has been very kind to me, and he is an admirable man. Upstanding, a great philanthropist and a credit to the community in every way. He is so admired for his charitable work. His work at Olave's is much esteemed, and he gives up his time selflessly – he's on the parole board at Holloway prison. People look up to him – everyone says that he is a pillar of the community."

"But, Grace, you're marrying a husband, not a pillar of the community."

"It's hard to explain, Rose. I have to think about Freddie, and what is best for his future. How I can best protect him."

She paused and looked at Aurora, her face wreathed in anxiety.

"Please don't take this the wrong way, Rory.

You know I love Edward dearly. But if Edward were more conventional, it would give Freddie all the protection he requires. But he's not. He's an actor. That in itself might not be a problem, but the Easingford name is already tainted by scandal, and the fact that Edward chooses to live beyond the rules that these people impose upon themselves makes the scandal linger."

Aurora nodded. "It's true. I can't enter a drawing room without hearing someone whisper the name Easingford and then start gossiping."

"I don't mind for myself," said Grace. "But I do mind for Freddie. He's being bullied at school. Badly, I think. I thought sending him away would be good for him in the longer term. I thought that if he grew up among these people, he would eventually be accepted as one of them. But he is ostracised. Sir Godfrey asked twice for my hand and I refused him because I didn't love him. But he is a governor at the school, and if I become Lady Caskins, it will afford Freddie all the protection he needs."

She saw the girls' shocked faces.

"Do you think I am being terribly wicked? I will be a good wife. I have promised myself I will be the best wife in the world to him." She gave a glum little smile and said brightly, "Besides, there's no getting out of it now. I've given my word to Sir Godfrey. And he is so kind – he sends flowers every day. If I were to break the engagement, it would only heap more scandal on the Easingford name."

"Does Edward know all this?" asked Aurora.

"Of course not," said Grace, "and neither of you must tell him."

"There is one solution," said Rose. "You and Freddie could just move to London, live here at Campion's and you could resume your music-hall career. Then what would it matter if it brought scandal to the Easingford name?"

"Ah," said Grace, "but you're forgetting Aurora and Edward. It might be hard on them."

"Well," said Rose gazing hard at Aurora, "there's a solution to that as well. They could change their names and move in too."

A look passed between Grace and Rory.

"Oh, Rose," said Grace. "If only it were that simple."

"I wish it were too," said Aurora fiercely. "Sometimes I feel trapped like a tiger in a net."

There was a sudden interruption as Inspector

Cliff and Billy arrived. They both shook hands with Thomas.

"Do you have news about Ivy's murder?" he asked eagerly. The Inspector shook his head and looked embarrassed. "Regrettably, no. Our lack of progress means we've been moved to the Plockton robbery. Quite a mystery that is proving to be too. But we had to come this way, so we thought that we would drop in because we have news for you, Rose. Billy was interviewing a former associate of the Duchess who had been arrested, and he asked her about Lizzie Gawkin. Seems she was quite a mine of information about Gawkin and her exploits. Apparently, some years ago Lizzie had been doing a job for the Duchess when she got distracted and stole a baby from a pram outside a theatre. Billy's informant didn't know who the baby belonged to, but she did know the name of the theatre where it happened – the Imperial Grand. What's more, she knew the name of the play that was on at the time – *The Winter's Tale.*"

There was a thud, and everyone turned. Perdita had fainted. Edward and some of the others went to her aid, but Rose stood immobile, as if she was made of ice. She could feel Thomas's hand on her shoulder. The Inspector, so delighted to be bringing the first concrete news to Rose of her mother, didn't notice her frozen features.

"The bad news," continued Cliff blithely, "is that the Imperial Grand burned down eleven years ago, and all its records were lost. But there must be someone still around working somewhere in London who recalls the names of those working on the production. I'm afraid Billy and I are too busy with the Fitzcillian and Plockton cases to give it our time, but it's the first solid lead you've ever had, and I thought you could do some investigation yourself..." He trailed off, seeing Rose's face.

"It's too late," she said dully. "I had news only yesterday. My mother is dead."

She burst into noisy tears and buried herself in Thomas's shoulder. When she looked up, everyone was starring at her, including Elenora de Valentina, who had materialised in the space as if by magic. She had a strange look on her face, as if satisfaction and sorrow were mingled.

14

Rose, Effie and Aurora were leaning over the balcony of the Victorious, a run-down hall in Clerkenwell that Rose thought might be better rechristened the Defeated. It was a place where those who were sliding down the bills of other music halls were to be found, as well as those just embarking on their careers. This was why the girls were there. Thomas had sent them to take a peek at a quartet of acrobats called the Tumbling Terrys, who he had heard were making a bit of a stir because of their daring routines.

But Rose wasn't in the mood. She had been unsettled by Elenora de Valentina's claim to have contacted her dead mother, and had been further upset by Inspector Cliff's news. Once, she would have been delighted to have the first solid lead on her mother's identity, although she didn't doubt how difficult it might be to find anyone who knew who she was after the passage of so much time. But although she had her suspicions about de Valentina's claims to communicate with the dead, she couldn't shake the troubling feeling that Inspector Cliff's information had come too late for her. Thomas had gently asked her if she would like him to make enquiries, but she had shaken her head and Thomas, seeing how close to tears she was, had not pressed the matter.

It didn't help that both Effie and Rory were treating Rose as if she was a very fragile glass vase that might shatter at any moment. She kept on catching them whispering together and looking at her anxiously. She simply pulled her coat around herself more tightly to protect against a vicious north wind and walked on gloomily. Normally she loved this time of the year – revelling in the approach of Christmas and its sights and smells. But she barely noticed the chestnut- and orange-sellers, and the spruce firs being sold, to be decorated with stars and candles at home. She had barely even responded when a cry had gone up as they walked over

London Bridge, and the girls had glanced back to see the tiger cub down on the shoreline, apparently playing with the mudlark children.

"Did you hear," asked Rory, "that Sir Godfrey sent a consignment of shoes for the mudlark families? It was nice of him to remember them when he's so far away."

"It was kind," said Effie. "There was a picture of the children wearing the shoes in the newspaper, and a write-up singing Sir Godfrey's praises as a great man. The writer said that he should stand for Parliament."

Rose said nothing. She had arrived at the Victorious in a glum mood, and was plunged further into gloom when she discovered that the Tumbling Terrys were way down the bill, and they would have to sit through several acts before them, including an appearance by Hopkin and Dent, who had been so disastrous during their single appearance at Campion's. Clearly their terrible Campion's appearance had also had an adverse impact on their career, if the Victorious was their best offer.

"We could go back outside and buy gingerbread," suggested Rory, but Rose was shivering with cold and shook her head.

"I want to stay here. We can watch Hopkin and Dent. Maybe they've improved."

"They can't have got worse," said Effie.

Hopkin and Dent came on stage soon after, and the girls leaned forward to watch closely. The stage went completely dark, and then suddenly two heads materialised, seemingly totally unattached to their bodies. The heads whizzed around the stage and the audience laughed, before the two heads bumped into each other and ended up at ground level. The effect was both spooky and silly, and the audience laughed even more appreciatively. Rose and the others looked at each other, puzzled. This was clever work, original and neatly put together. Both men were now visible – rotund figures, dapperly dressed in sombre suits and each holding a cane. But what made the audience gasp and clap was that both of them appeared to be completely headless. Then the headless men began tap-dancing, and the audience laughed and clapped with pleasure.

When the act finished, Rose looked at the others. They were all perplexed. Hopkin and Dent had been excellent – nothing like the stumbling, bumbling performance they had put in on their first and last night at Campion's. On the evidence of what she had just seen, if Rose had been sent to scout them she would recommend them to Thomas without hesitation. Yet when they had played Campion's they had appeared so lacking in competence that the Campion's audience had taken violently against them. If Thomas hadn't stopped the act when he did, some of the more unruly members of the audience would have started throwing the furniture at them.

"It's so odd," said Effie. "You would barely know it was the same act."

Rose nodded her agreement. "I always thought it was strange they were so bad. They came to Campion's highly recommended. There must be a reason why they were so terrible on that night and so impressive today." A gleam came into her eyes. "There's no harm in asking them."

So after they had watched the acrobats, and agreed that Thomas should make them a modest offer to start at Campion's after the pantomime season, they went round to the stage door and asked for Hopkin and Dent. They were pointed towards a door at the end of the corridor, knocked and were told to enter. As soon as Mr Hopkin saw Rose and Effie he looked embarrassed, like a schoolboy caught filching sweets. Mr Dent suddenly developed a nervous twitch in his left eye, which made him look as if he was winking at the girls.

"We just came to say how much we enjoyed your act tonight," said Rose.

"You did?" said Mr Dent, and it came out as a yelp.

"We did," said Effie. "We were impressed."

"Yes," said Rose. "We were. But we were also very curious as to why, when you can be this good, you were so blooming awful on your one and only night at Campion's."

"Rose!" said Aurora, shocked by her friend's directness.

"I'm only asking," said Rose, "because it's such a puzzle. It was your big break. Why throw it away like that? You could have been top of the bill at Campion's for weeks. Instead you bottled it, and now you're here."

The men seemed anxious, darting little meaningful glances at each other.

"Yes, now we're here," muttered Mr Hopkin, casting his eye mournfully around the down-at-heel dressing room with its bare boards and cracked mirror. "But at least we're alive."

"Hopkin!" said the other man warningly, and his tic twitched alarmingly.

There was something about the duo that reminded Rose of Tweedledee and Tweedledum, the characters from *Lewis Carroll's Through the Looking-Glass*. Rose thought back to the duo's performance at Campion's. She remembered describing them as being as jumpy as cats. She had thought that they had simply been suffering from terrible stage fright, but after seeing them perform tonight that seemed an unlikely explanation. They had been confident and in control on stage – it was only now that they seemed tense and panicky. And it wasn't just nerves: if Rose had to make a guess, she would say that both of these men were afraid of something. She recalled that Thomas had said that after their terrible performance at Campion's, they had left the theatre with such haste it was as if they were being pursued by all the demons of hell.

"Look," she said. "I imagine you would love to get out of the Victorious and play somewhere more salubrious. Well, we could help you. You were really good today, but I'm guessing that few of the better halls will have you after your Campion's disaster. Word travels fast." Both men nodded. "But I could tell Thomas how good you were, and maybe get him to come and see you himself. And perhaps he could put in a good word for you with some of the other hall owners." The men looked eager. "But I can only help you if you are honest with me. You are both afraid of something, aren't you? What was it that frightened you so much that you deliberately threw your act at Campion's so badly that you've become virtually unemployable? Nobody does that to their own career unless they are very, very scared."

The men looked at each other and seemed to come to a decision. Hopkin gave a nod. Dent went to a small box, took a key from his pocket and unlocked it. He withdrew a folded sheet of paper and passed it to Rose. She opened it up. The words, written in a fine copperplate hand, said: "Be warned. If you play another night at Campion's, both of you will die. This is no joke. Remember Desiree, and take note. Your names are already on the bullets."

Hopkin opened his hand. "These were

delivered with the note." In his palm were two bullets. Rose held them up to the light. On one was engraved a "D", and on the other, an "H".

* ✳ *

Rose ran up the stairs at Campion's. She wanted to tell Thomas about their encounter with Hopkin and Dent. She was furious that the investigation into the murder of poor Ivy had been downgraded because of the Fitzcillian and Plockton robberies – as if the loss of a few jewels by the rich was of greater importance than the death of a poor music-hall dancer – and so, on their way back from the Victorious, they had made a detour to Scotland Yard. There they had delivered the threatening note and the bullets into the hands of Inspector Cliff, who had agreed that it was new evidence. But there was something in his manner that made Rose think that Ivy's death was still not going to be an immediate priority.

She, Effie and Rory had discussed what they knew on their way back, but none of them could come up with a reason why somebody would kill Ivy and then threaten to do the same to Hopkin and Dent.

"There has to be something that connects the

two of them," said Rose. "But when I asked them, Hopkin and Dent said they had never met Ivy, and I don't think they were lying."

"Me neither," said Rory drily, who thought that by the end of their interrogation by Rose it was hard to know if Hopkin and Dent were more scared of her or the unknown person who had written the note. They had passed it and the bullets over to Rose with barely a murmur.

"There must be something else that connects them – something that got Ivy killed, and Hopkin and Dent threatened to the point they felt their lives were at risk."

"Yes," said Effie. "The bullets were a particularly macabre touch."

"A dramatic flourish," said Aurora.

"A very effective one," said Rose. She was still thinking about it as she climbed the stairs towards Thomas's study. She went to put her hand on the door when she realised she could hear voices coming from inside. She paused, her hand on the handle.

She heard Thomas ask, "I assume you have ensured that the emeralds are Grace's, and belong to Grace alone, and in no circumstances can be claimed by Sir Godfrey."

"Of course, I have taken legal advice. She will own them entirely in her own right," said Edward.

Rose turned to go back downstairs. Thomas and Edward were clearly deep in conversation. Now was not the moment to disturb them with her discovery about Hopkin and Dent.

But then Edward added, "I would not say that Sir Godfrey was delighted by the news, when I told him that I would be settling the emeralds on Grace, and that he would have no claim over them. He said it would look to the world as if I did not entirely trust him."

"And do you?" asked Thomas.

"I can't say I warm to the man, and I have no earthly idea what Grace sees in him that makes her want to marry him. But he is very widely regarded and has an impeccable reputation for his good works with the poor and needy. He sits on numerous charity committees and he's always telling people about how much of his own money he has donated to the poor. So it's not as if he needs the emeralds. In any case, I had already agreed to give him a substantial dowry – a dowry of which Grace is unaware and which I for one will ensure she never knows about."

Rose knew she shouldn't listen any further, but she paused on the stairs, digesting this piece of information. A dowry! Sir Godfrey was effectively being paid to marry Grace. It was almost medieval.

"Did he ask for one before he proposed?" asked Thomas, sounding concerned.

"Not in so many words," continued Edward. "He danced around the subject, as only a gentleman of his class and background can, but his meaning was quite clear. He said that the money would be used entirely for charitable purposes."

Rose crept down the stairs. Her brain was buzzing. No wonder Sir Godfrey had been so persistent in his proposals. She wondered if Grace would have ever said yes if she had known about the dowry. She was in such a daze she didn't notice Perdita waiting for her at the bottom of the stairs.

"Rose," she said conspiratorially. "I just wanted to check that you are none the worse for wear after our adventure the other night."

"I'm fine – but are you quite recovered from your faint, Perdita?"

"It was nothing. I had simply failed to eat

any breakfast," said Perdita, but she looked pale and anxious. She put her arm around Rose's shoulder in a motherly fashion and held her tight, as if she feared she might get away. "I wasn't just thinking of your encounter with that unpleasant young man. I heard about the message from beyond the grave that Madame de Valentina had for you at Lant Street. It must have been unsettling."

Rose nodded. "It was. I don't know what to believe. I don't really think she can talk to the dead and yet ... yet..." Rose found herself crying. "I can't help feeling she may be right, and my mother is dead. I want to believe that my mother is out there somewhere, and has never given up hope that she will find me. But in truth, I know that she is probably long dead." Perdita enveloped Rose in her arms, and for a moment Rose imagined it was her mother's embrace. She allowed herself to relax into them as she sobbed quietly.

"So," said Perdita softly. "Are you going to follow up on the Inspector's information?"

"I don't see the point," said Rose. "It doesn't matter what Elenora says – in my heart I know my mother is dead. And if I'm wrong, and she isn't, maybe she doesn't want to be found. So why bother?"

"You must do what you think best," said Perdita.

After a few seconds the pair broke apart, and when Rose looked up she saw tears in Perdita's eyes. She glanced behind them and saw Ella watching them from the end of corridor, with a look on her face that had the furtiveness of a spy – but which was also full of longing.

15

Rose, Effie and Aurora hurried back over London Bridge towards Campion's for one last rehearsal of the pantomime before *Cinderella* opened later that night. They had been at Silver Square with Aurora, where they had tried on the frocks that they might wear for the dinner when Grace would be presented with the Easingford Emeralds in two days' time.

It was another bitterly cold day. Curdled grey clouds bearing more snow hung sullenly in the sky, but there was a real whiff of Christmas in the air too – the scent of roasting chestnuts, and cloves and cinnamon, drifting across the bridge from the stalls selling mulled ale. Rose was feeling much better and had a spring in her step. In some ways she wondered whether

Madame de Valentina might have done her a favour. All her life, since she was still a little girl and Thomas had explained to her how she had been found on the steps of Campion's, she had thought obsessively about her lost mother. Not a day had passed when she hadn't dreamed about finding her. Madame de Valentina may have been faking it when she said that she was communicating with the spirit of Rose's mother, but even if it was a lie, Rose felt it had made her face up to reality: she was never going to feel a mother's embrace. She just had to get on with her life.

Perhaps it made it easier to be grateful for what she did have: Thomas's warm, unconditional love, a home at Campion's that she adored, and all the warmth and friendship of the Campion's family. So many of those working at Campion's were, like poor dead Ivy, entirely without ties. Some were estranged from their families and others, like Rose, had never known them, or lost them at some point along the way. She was not unusual. The streets of London were full of orphaned children who hadn't had her luck to be abandoned on the steps of Campion's and found by someone as caring and tender-hearted as Thomas. She knew she was fortunate, and from now on she resolved to stop daydreaming about her mother and instead appreciate her good luck.

The girls stopped to buy chestnuts, and across the bridge Rose saw John, the eldest Tanner Street boy, looking at them. Very slowly, Rose met his insolent stare with a grin, and in a nimble gesture raised her hand and pointed it at him like a pistol. He dropped his eyes and skulked away. Rose suspected she would have no further trouble from him.

"What was that all about?" asked Effie, who had noticed the fleeting encounter and Rose's odd gesture.

"Nothing," said Rose.

"The Tanner Street boys haven't been bothering you since they were banned? If they have, you should tell Thomas sharpish," said Rory.

"Oh, I don't think they will be any further trouble," said Rose. She knew that John wouldn't want his encounter with Perdita to become common knowledge around Southwark. It would make him a laughing stock and do nothing for his hard-man reputation. "In fact, I may ask Thomas to give the Tanner Street boys an early Christmas present and un-ban them. They've never missed a Campion's pantomime. There was one year when a couple of the youngest of them tried to storm the stage mid-performance to have a ride on the panto horse. It was very funny."

They walked on further past the stalls and the homeless beggars asking for alms who huddled along the side of the bridge. Suddenly Rose broke step, and turned and walked back a short distance, stopping by two small figures sitting on the ground hunched against the cold. She bent down.

"It's Florrie and Col, isn't it?" she asked. The pair nodded miserably. The last time Rose had seen them they were up on the stage at Campion's, having been summoned there by Madame de Valentina – willing participants, or victims, depending on your point of view, thought Rose – in her hypnotism act. Then the youngsters had had a glow about them; they had been flushed with love and optimism. Florrie's hair had been glossy, and Col had looked spruce. Now Florrie's hair was lank, and Col had the frayed look of one who had been living on the streets for several days. Effie and Rory had walked back to join them.

"What are you doing here? What about your positions at Lady Plockton's?" asked Rose, appalled by their transformation.

"We were let go," whispered Florrie. "After the robbery."

Rose frowned. "But why? Surely if the police think you were involved in any way, they would have arrested you?"

"Mud sticks," said Col gloomily. "Two of the other servants said that Florrie wasn't in her bed on the night of the robbery, and because the police think it was an inside job, of course it looks suspicious."

"And were you up and about in the middle of the night?" asked Aurora.

Florrie shook her head and her face crumpled. "If I was, I can't remember it. As far as I know I went to bed at ten o'clock, fell fast asleep and woke up again at five o' clock in the morning, when I was called to make up the fires. All I can recall is that I had a dream in which I heard a bell ringing. But Nancy and Jane swear blind that they were both awake during the night and that my bed was empty. They thought about coming to look for me. Even worse, it was around the time that the police think the robbery took place."

"Do these girls have any kind of grudge against you?" asked Rose.

Florrie shook her head and tears ran down her cheeks. "No, that's the horrible thing. They were both my friends. We all stuck by each other."

"You don't think they've got a reason to lie – that they could have been involved in the robbery in some way?"

Florrie shook her head again. "They were the sweetest, most truthful girls, as honest as the day. Before this happened, I'd have trusted them with my life."

"So how did you end up on the streets?" asked Effie.

"The butler sent for me and said I was to be let go on the orders of Lady Plockton herself. Without references."

Rose felt anger well inside her gut. You were supposed to be innocent until found guilty, and Florrie hadn't even been arrested, let alone charged with a crime. Yet being let go without references was a punishment that would follow poor Florrie for the rest of her life. She would never find another position without references.

"He said it was regrettable, but that Lady Plockton did not trust to have me in the house. I was made to leave immediately."

"What about you, Col?" asked Rose, turning to the boy. His face was one of pure outrage.

"The butler called me in and said that if I wanted to keep my job I was never to see or have any contact with Florrie again." He took Florrie's hand and clutched it tight. "But I know my Florrie. I know that she is no thief, so I walked out with her there and then."

With no references either, thought Rose. She admired the boy's loyalty to Florrie, but loyalty wasn't going to help them eat for the next fifty years.

"Have you no family to take you in?" asked Rose.

"Mine are all dead. Florrie only has her dad, and he's a demon when he drinks, and he drinks whenever he has money in his pocket," said Col. "I've tried to get work. First few days I walked all over the city. But now we have to store up our energy against the cold." He gave a cough – a nasty, painful sound.

"So there's no one you can turn to?"

"I have an aunt – my late mother's sister," said Florrie. "She lives in Shadwell. She might provide shelter. She rents a little house there. Her husband was the stage-doorkeeper at the Imperial Grand before he died of the consumption, just before the place burned down."

"The Imperial Grand?" asked Rose sharply.

"Yes," said Florrie. "He was there for the fifteen years before he died. When I was a little girl he used to tell me about all the shows and the actors and actresses who appeared in them. He knew all the gossip."

For a moment Rose allowed her mind to drift. She was talking to somebody who had known somebody who had almost certainly known her mother. So close. Yet so far.

"Did he ever mention a production of *The Winter's Tale*, and an incident with a baby going missing during the run?"

Florrie shook her head. "If he did, I don't remember."

A blast of arctic air howled over the bridge, and Col's hacking cough brought Rose back to the situation in hand.

"So why can't you stay at your aunt's?" she asked.

"She's not there," said Florrie. "House is all locked up. I asked a neighbour. Said she had gone to visit her late husband's sister in Tunbridge Wells. She may not be back until after Christmas."

Rose stood up and held out a hand to Florrie, pulling her up.

"Come on. You are coming back to Campion's with us. With the pantomime starting tonight, we'll need all the extra help we can get. Florrie can top-to-tail with me, and Col can kip down behind the bar. We'll send a note over to your aunt's house to find on her return and tell her where you are."

"We don't want to be any trouble," said Col.

"You're not trouble," said Rose firmly. She waved an arm at the other huddled figures on the bridge. "The trouble's not you – it's that we live in a city where some have so much and many have so little. Come on, don't dawdle, there will be hot pies at Campion's, and a fire."

They arrived back at Campion's just as Madame de Valentina was arriving to do the early show. Tonight, the panto was top of the bill, at the end of the second show of the night, but it wouldn't run every show, or every day, ensuring that those who wanted to see Madam de Valentina's act would still have plenty of opportunity to do so. She was still drawing a huge crowd, with her heady mix of hypnotism and conversations with the dead, although Rose had noticed that this part of her act was getting ever shorter.

She swept towards the stage door, already dressed for her performance as she always was, arriving and leaving in the same clothes that she wore on stage. Rose and the others had talked about how odd it was. For most hall folk, changing clothes and getting into a costume and ready for a performance marked the division between reality and the theatre. They needed the moment of transformation, both before the show and then after it. But Elenora wore the same clothes on stage as she did off it, which made Rose wonder whether her entire life was one big act, for which she was always wearing a costume. There was something about Elenora's invincible confidence, as she put her hand on the stage door handle, that made Rose call out to her.

"Ah, Madame de Valentina. I'm sure you remember Florrie and Col."

Elenora turned and peered at them uncertainly. Rose prompted her. "Your first night here at Campion's you brought them up on stage and hypnotised them."

Elenora gave a vague smile. "Of course," she said. "Florrie and Col. You work at Lady Plockton's, I believe."

"They did," said Rose. "But they lost their jobs after the robbery. Suspicion fell on them and they were treated as guilty and flung out on the streets, even though nothing had been proved against them, and they haven't even been arrested."

Elenora looked pained. "Poor innocent lambs," she said. "What a dreadful thing to happen." She seemed genuinely distressed. "Excuse me. I must prepare for my performance."

16

Rose and Ella were standing at the back of the auditorium, watching Madame de Valentina's act. Campion's looked beautiful. There was a Christmas tree by the bar, and Ella had attached holly and mistletoe to the mirrors all around the auditorium. Thomas had found her a set of silver bells from the prop cupboard and she had tied them up the slender, gilt-painted pillars that supported the horseshoe balcony. The bells winked through the haze from the gas lights, creating a festive air.

Campion's was already packed, and many of those who were here for the early show would be staying on to see the pantomime. Thomas predicted that it might be one of the music hall's most profitable evenings, before adding wryly,

195

"Which is probably just as well, if you are going to keep inviting all of London's waifs and strays to join us, Rose."

"Not all," said Rose. "There are still thousands out there every bit as needy as Ella, Florrie and Col. Besides," she added, "Ella has turned out to be a small miracle in the kitchen. She more than pays her way."

Thomas nodded. "She's worth her weight in gold. A lovely woman, clearly educated too. I don't know what happened to her, but it must be something bad for her to have ended up destitute. She seems to know a thing or two about stagecraft too. It was Ella who suggested I change that bit in the walkdown at the end with Dandini, and she was quite right – it is much better."

Rose gave Thomas a sideways look. It wasn't normal for him to be taking directing advice from the kitchen staff. Now she thought about it, there had been a couple of occasions when she had seen Thomas and Ella deep in conversation together. From what he said it didn't sound as if Thomas had found out any more about her and how she had ended up at Campion's kitchen door than Rose herself. Ella was like an oyster that refused to be prised open.

"Actually," continued Thomas, "I reckon she's wasted washing up. I was thinking about asking her to stay on permanently and take over running the bar."

"It would be wonderful if she would stay," said Rose.

"You don't think she will?" asked Thomas, and he sounded disappointed.

"I don't know," said Rose, "but I somehow got the impression when she appeared like magic and saved me from a night in the kitchen that she saw the kitchen job as being temporary. But I may be wrong. Perhaps if you can give her a good reason to stay she will."

"Ah," said Thomas. "Then we will just have to find a very good reason."

Now, with Florrie and Col helping out in the kitchen, Rose had beckoned Ella into the auditorium, so that she would get to see Madame de Valentina's act in full for the first time.

"I'll be interested to know what you think, Ella," said Rose. Then she added lightly, "By the way, do you know Perdita from the past somewhere? I thought from your reaction at the rehearsal the other day that you might have recognised her."

Ella smiled. "You don't miss anything, do you, Rose Campion. Yes, I thought I recognised her, but I quickly realised that she is quite a different woman from the one I once knew."

Ella's body language made it quite clear that this particular conversation was at an end.

"I think Thomas hopes you might decide to stay on with us," said Rose. Ella said nothing. "Campion's is a good place to call home," Rose continued. "I should know. Thomas gave me one."

"I heard that you were found abandoned on the steps of the music hall as a baby."

"Yes," said Rose. "I'm part of Campion's legend."

"How old are you now, Rose?"

"Twelve. I'll be thirteen on January the first. Of course, nobody knows my exact birthday, but I was only a few weeks old when I was found."

Ella's eyes had filled with tears, and she put a hand out to Rose and brushed her cheek with her fingers.

"I'm glad you found happiness, Rose. I wish all lost children could be as lucky as you."

Madame de Valentina had begun her act. Ella

stood with her eyes fixed on Elenora. It was early on in the act, and Elenora was doing a card trick. Rose's sharp eyes detected a tiny fumble, and from Ella's reaction beside her, she knew she had spotted it too. Rose was surprised. It was rare for a member of the public to spot a mistake in a magic act. The public were so willing to be deceived that even when the performer did make a slip, it was unusual that the audience noticed.

Madame de Valentina had moved on to the part of her act when she picked someone from the audience and got them to come up on stage to be hypnotised. De Valentina's attention was on a dapper young man in the audience who, with much ribbing from his friends, was being called up on stage. He was a footman at the Duke of Dover's house in Cardigan Square.

Rose thought she'd better slip back into the kitchen to check that Florrie and Col were getting on all right. The cook had a reputation for being fearsome, although he purred like a pussycat whenever Ella was near. "I'll be back in a minute," she whispered to Ella.

Even with the back door open on such a cold night, the kitchen was like a furnace.

Rose wedged the door between the kitchen and auditorium open to try and get a through-draught going for a few minutes.

"Hot enough?" she asked Florrie and Col, who were working together to tackle the teetering tower of dirty crockery and saucepans.

Florrie grinned and wiped her sweaty forehead with her sleeve.

"I never thought I'd complain again about being too hot after sitting on that freezing bridge, but it is roasting in here."

"It is," said Col. "And it's blissful. I feel better already."

"We've just had good news too," said Florrie. "A messenger came. My aunt has returned home. She got the note you arranged to be sent and asked us to come first thing tomorrow. She said we could stay with her as long as we need to, until we find new positions."

"That's wonderful," said Rose.

They both looked so happy that she didn't like to say how hard it might be for them to find jobs that in any way matched their ones at Lady Plockton's.

There was a mew at the door and Ophelia sauntered in, closely followed by the tiger cub.

The tiger had grown enormously. It made a little snorting sound, as if trying to say hello. Rose picked up two slices of raw beef and, with one in each hand, she held them out to the cat and the tiger. Unused to such largesse, Ophelia snatched her piece between her teeth and ran outside, as if fearing that Rose might change her mind, but the tiger took the meat directly from Rose's hand and then sat expectantly waiting for another slice, which Rose gave it. She stroked the cub's head as it ate. It purred loudly. She pointed to the back door with her free hand and nodded to Florrie to pass her a piece of rope hanging on the handle, in the hope that she might be able loop it over the tiger's head. She was confident that the Tanner Street boys had given up on their attempts to catch the tiger, but there were plenty more out there with an eye on its skin. She hated the idea of the beautiful creature being behind bars, but she knew Thomas was right when he said that the only safe place for it in London was the Zoological Gardens in Regent's Park. Florrie reached for the rope and started towards Rose and the tiger, walking carefully so as not to frighten the animal.

There was a roar of laughter from the hall,

and then the audience fell silent, and the distant tinkle of Madame de Valentina's bell drifted into the kitchen. Florrie, still a few feet from Rose, suddenly stood stock-still, her eyes glazed.

"Florrie," hissed Rose, gesturing her to hand her the rope. But the girl didn't move.

"Florrie!" said Col grabbing her arm.

But still the girl stood frozen, as if she was a statue. Rose frowned, and Col looked frightened. There was another roar of laughter from the auditorium, and the tiger, alarmed by the sound, slipped from Rose's grasp and bounded out of the door. The auditorium quietened, and Madame de Valentina rang her little silver bell again. The audience began to clap, and Florrie unfroze, looked down at the rope in her hand as if perplexed, and asked, "What am I doing?"

Gently, Col took the rope from her hand, and Florrie grinned brightly at him and returned briskly to the sink, as if nothing had happened.

"Florrie, are you all right?" asked Rose.

The girl turned around. "I'm fine. Why shouldn't I be?" She saw Rose and Col staring at her. "What is it?" she asked, looking scared.

"It was just that you froze, Floss. It was as

if you had turned into a statue. You were here but you weren't here, as if your mind had been spirited away. Like a trance."

Florrie laughed. "You are both having me on." She saw their faces and looked frightened again.

"It was probably nothing," said Rose. "We all get distracted. Maybe that's all it was." She turned to Col. "Have you ever seen Florrie like that before?"

He shook his head.

Rose gave a cheery smile. "So that probably means there is nothing to worry about."

But she did think it was odd. Florrie's momentary lack of responsiveness, and the glazed eyes, had been spooky.

Leaving Florrie and Tom to their task, she returned to Ella's side at the back of the auditorium where Madame de Valentina was just finishing the last part of her act, during which she claimed to communicate with the dead. Rose could see Pru back in the audience, as she was almost every night, hanging on to Elenora's every word and still hoping for another message from her mother, even though Madame de Valentina had warned her that there would be no further communications. The communing with the dead part of the act was over quickly, and the audience was vocal in its disappointment. Rose thought it was odd. It was that part of the act that most of the audience were there for – almost everyone had someone they had lost and longed to communicate with one last time. Most music-hall artistes shaped their act to deliver what the audience wanted, but Elenora didn't seem to be bothered. It made Rose wonder if Madame de Valentina was going to leave Campion's quite soon. The act came to an end; the audience stamped and shrieked its approval. But Ella didn't even clap.

"What do you think?" asked Rose curiously.

"An amateur," said Ella crisply.

"Did you ever work in the theatre?" asked Rose.

"In another life, yes," said Ella softly. "But that life was stolen from me. Maybe one day I will get it back again." She walked away to the kitchen.

Thomas came and stood beside Rose.

"Shouldn't you be backstage getting ready for the pantomime?"

Rose nodded. "I'm just on my way."

"I'll come with you," said Thomas. "I need

to talk to Madame de Valentina before she vanishes into the night. I've just had a note from Sir Godfrey. He's returning to London in the morning and suggested some entertainment before the dinner at Silver Square tomorrow night. He wants me to ask Madame de Valentina if she will perform the hypnotism part of her act. I fear he will be disappointed. She may be hard to persuade."

"I'm sure you'll manage, Thomas," said Rose. "Her mind may rule the world, but yours rules Campion's."

17

Rose and the rest of the *Cinderella* cast took one final bow and rushed off stage, hugging each other. The pantomime was a clear hit with the audience. They had booed Rose and Rory's Ugly Sisters with gusto, laughed at Edward's Baroness Hard-Up, gasped when Grace – under the alias Miss Jenny Roberts – had swooped across the stage as Prince Charming, and cried when Dolores' Cinderella tried on the shoe and it fitted. They had loved the magical moment at the end of the show, when fake snow started to fall from above – an idea that had come from Effie, and which involved thousands of tiny cut-up pieces of paper suspended in a net above the stage. She had spent hours working with the stage hands to get it right. There would be a lot of sweeping up in the morning, but it was worth it for the delight on the audience's faces.

Rose couldn't wait to get out of her costume, thick make-up and wig, and go back into the auditorium, where there would be a huge party for everyone who worked at Campion's, as soon as the last members of the public had been ushered from the building. It was always one of the jolliest evenings of the year and much anticipated.

"That was one of the best nights of my life," said Grace, removing her dark wig to reveal her blonde curls and peeling off the leather boots that extended right to her thigh.

"You could have plenty more like it," said Rose. "All you have to do is tell Sir Godfrey you've changed your mind about marrying him."

Grace shook her head. "I couldn't do that to the poor man."

Not so poor, thought Rose to herself – not with the dowry that Edward was giving to him. She wondered if Grace would change her mind if she knew.

"Well done, everyone," said Thomas, beaming. "Another Campion's pantomime triumph.

Those Tanner Street boys said they thought it was the best one yet." He raised an eyebrow. "And of course that is the highest praise possible. John said he was delighted he hadn't put a match to the place, because he wouldn't have missed it for the world."

Rose smiled. She was pleased that Thomas had lifted the ban. The Tanner Street boys may be trouble, but they were as much a part of the weft and weave of Campion's daily life as Lottie, Dolores and O'Leary. It was better to embrace them, warts and all, than try to keep them out. They belonged at Campion's in a way that none of the toffs who made the journey south across the river would ever be able to claim.

There had been plenty of toffs in tonight, and Rose wondered just how shocked they would have been if they'd realised that it was Grace Easingford, shortly to be the wife of the upstanding Godfrey Caskins, who had played Prince Charming so delightfully, soaring across the stage like a bird, her legs exposed above her boots. But she was confident that both Grace and Aurora were unrecognisable in their costumes, and if anyone voiced suspicions they would be strenuously denied.

The party had begun. Jem, part of the Campion's company, was playing the fiddle and most people were dancing. Everyone who worked at Campion's was there, apart from Madame de Valentina, who had departed straight after her act as usual, vanishing into the night. Even Pru had stayed on, and she was dancing with a smile on her face – the first real one since her mother's sudden death. Rose had tried to persuade Ella to join them, but she had said that she was tired and would prefer to stay in the kitchen.

"You must be the only Cinderella who doesn't want to go to the ball," said Rose with a grin, and although it made Ella smile, she said, "I am quite content here on my own," and she picked up her book. Rose noticed that she was reading *The Winter's Tale*.

"I love that play. Maybe it's because I'm a lost baby myself."

"It's wonderful," replied Ella, "and so true about how jealousy can lead to great loss." Then she added, "The past cannot be undone. But we can forgive, and be redeemed. Off you go, Rose. Enjoy yourself. And have a dance for me."

As she danced with Aurora and Effie, Rose

thought about *The Winter's Tale* and its story of a mother and child separated and lost to each other. Maybe she should follow up on the information that Inspector Cliff had given her. She looked around the room at the sea of happy faces. Only a few were standing or sitting at the margins. Perdita was one of them, sitting alone in a seat in the shadows, where she could observe the party without participating in it. On several occasions, Rose looked up to find Perdita's eyes fixed on her, a pensive look on her face. Rose thought about trying to drag her into the circle of dancers, but decided against it. You couldn't make people join in the dance if they didn't want to, and there was something about Perdita's stance that suggested she would be resistant, although the longing in her eyes told another story. Rose thought it was almost as if Perdita was punishing herself in some way.

After a while she, Effie and Rory were so hot that they headed for the stage door so that they could stand in the yard and enjoy the freezing air. O'Leary was sitting at the stage door dozing, content with half a bottle of brandy by his side. He woke up with a jump as they passed.

"Hello, girls. Enjoying yourselves?"

"Yes, we just came for a breath of air."

"On your way back, can you give that to Miss Grace," said O'Leary, pointing to a small spray of white carnations held together by a pin, on to which was secured a single diamond earring. A note addressed to Miss Jenny Roberts was also attached.

"Pretty," observed Rose, picking up the spray. As she did so the note fell open. Written in copperplate script were the words, "A gift for Jenny, a beautiful little tiger, from the tiger hunter. Meet me at midnight on the steps of St Paul's Cathedral if you would like the second earring. Look for a white carnation."

"O'Leary," asked Rose urgently. "Who delivered this and when?"

O'Leary shrugged. "A messenger boy. About an hour ago."

"What's wrong, Rose?" asked Effie.

Rose held up the note so Effie and Rory could both read it. They gasped.

"It's very similar to the note that was delivered with Ivy's tiger," said Effie.

"It is," said Rose. "And the earring is just like the ones I saw Ivy wearing, shortly before she was shot. Maybe whoever sent this note was also the person who killed Ivy."

"Well, Grace can't possibly go," said Rory.

"No, she can't," said Rose. "But we can."

* ✳ *

The city was wrapped in a cloak of darkness, the few lamps still lit revealing glittering frosted streets. Rose, Effie and Rory made their way cautiously – slip-sliding despite their sturdy boots – through the narrow passages behind St Paul's. It was close to midnight. They crept down an alley that would bring them out close to the steps leading up to the front entrance of the great cathedral. Aurora had been doubtful about the plan, suggesting they should get Thomas involved from the start.

"And shouldn't we tell Grace about the note? It was sent to her, after all," she had said, a frown on her face.

"It would spoil the party," Rose had said firmly, and watching Grace whirl around the room with such undisguised pleasure, Aurora had to agree it would be a pity to ruin the evening for her.

"Why worry her half to death, when we can go to St Paul's, discover who the stranger is who sent the note and apprehend them ourselves? There are three of us and only one of him. Besides, we will have the advantage of surprise. Whoever he is, he won't be expecting us. Anyway, we can call for help if we need it."

"But if he's a toff, as seems likely from the diamond earring, he will have much more authority than us. We're more likely to be the ones to be arrested," said Effie, looking worried.

"And how much help will there be around at the dead of night anyway? And if he does a runner, what will we do?" asked Rory.

"Chase him," said Rose. "We're bound to be younger, fitter and faster. At the very worst we'll be able to give the police a good description of him, and at least now we've got some evidence," she added, holding up the note and earring.

They approached the great cathedral, their boots crunching on the packed ice. Aurora had been wrong in her worry about there being nobody around. Despite the chill, there were plenty of people in the vicinity, although Rose suspected that many of them were engaged in business that they preferred to do under the cloak of darkness. There were also a number of homeless people huddled in the precincts of the church, and down a narrow alley, a brazier had been lit, and the faces of those standing around were ruddy in the glow from the flames. They were singing carols.

They slowed down to take stock and plan their approach. Rose had assumed that their quarry would be alone and visible from a distance. But there were a surprising number of people, as well as several dogs, milling around at the top of the stairs, and she realised that whoever was trying to lure Grace here had sought safety in numbers. Maybe this was a well-known place for midnight assignations? Leaning against one of the columns, a man and a woman were kissing passionately, and at the top of stairs there were several men standing alone, as if they were each waiting for somebody. From the way they were dressed, it was clear that most of them were gentlemen. But none of them appeared to have a white carnation.

The girls decided to stay where they were positioned, at the bottom of the stairs to the left, where they were less obviously visible. The moon had escaped from behind a cloud, and they had a good view of the people on the steps. The cathedral's newly installed clock began to chime the midnight hour. As the last note died away, a new figure emerged from behind one of the columns at the top of the stairs. He was wearing a top hat, and a white carnation was clearly visible in his buttonhole. He pushed his hat up, making his face visible. The girls gasped. The man wasn't a stranger: it was Sir Godfrey Caskins.

18

Rose, Effie and Aurora were at Silver Square, getting ready for the dinner to celebrate Grace's forthcoming marriage to Sir Godfrey. It was almost seven o'clock. Madame de Valentina was already downstairs, preparing her act in the Chinese drawing room, where the pre-dinner entertainment would take place, and the guests would shortly be arriving.

"What on earth are we going to do?" asked Aurora, as she tried to do up the hooks and eyes at the back of Rose's dress. She was all fingers and thumbs, and Rose was so consumed with anxiety that she could barely stand still. Effie was biting her fingernails and kept darting back and forth to the window to peer out.

They had raced as fast as the icy streets would

allow them back to Campion's, ready to tell Grace, Thomas and Edward what they had discovered. But when they arrived back they had discovered that the party was over early because a message had come, summoning Grace to the Hampshire school where Freddie was a pupil. He had suffered an accident. Thomas and Edward had immediately set off with Grace, leaving a note explaining what had happened, and promising to be in touch with further news in the morning about whether or not the dinner, at which the Easingford Emeralds would be presented to Grace, would go ahead.

Although the girls were worried about Freddie, the news that the dinner might be cancelled had come as something of a relief, making the need to tell Grace about Sir Godfrey's behaviour less pressing. In the morning, Thomas had sent another note, saying that Freddie's accident was less serious than initially feared and that they would be returning to London by late afternoon.

"Which will at least give us time to show them the note and earring and tell them about seeing Sir Godfrey at St Paul's," said Rose.

But late afternoon had come and gone, and it had been followed by another note to say that the party had been caught in a snowstorm but would be back before the first guests arrived. But that was now looking increasingly unlikely too.

"You don't think," asked Aurora, "that Sir Godfrey could possibly have known that 'Jenny' is really Grace?"

Effie shook her head. "I don't. Even some of Campion's regulars are unaware that Pru and Belle Canterbury are one and the same person. The leap from Grace to Prince Charming is an even greater one."

"No," agreed Rose. "The disguise is far too good."

"It is," said Effie. "I'm confident of that. It's far more likely that Sir Godfrey was simply tickled by a pretty face and thought he'd try his luck, as he had with Ivy."

"I knew he looked familiar – and that he was lying when he claimed that he had never been to Campion's before on the night Ivy died," said Rose.

"It was a risky thing to do though," said Effie. "You might have called him out on it if you had been more certain you had seen him there before."

"It was even more risky to slip in to see the pantomime last night. Any one of us might have seen and recognised him," said Rose.

"Much less so if he took a little care over his appearance and was up in the gallery," said Rory. "But maybe taking the risk is part of the thrill for him. Perhaps he enjoys getting away with it, knowing the world sees him in one way, when privately he behaves in quite another."

"Maybe shooting music-hall stars is just another form of thrill for him," said Rose darkly. "Like big-game hunting."

"But did he shoot Ivy?" asked Effie. "We can't jump to conclusions. We've got the evidence of our own eyes that Sir Godfrey is a hypocrite – engaged to Grace and yet seeking dalliances with other women – but we don't know that he is a murderer. He may well have formed a relationship with Ivy but that doesn't mean he killed her. He may well have been very fond of her."

"But somebody did kill Ivy," said Rose, "and he's the obvious suspect."

"Maybe you're right," said Effie. "But what was his motive?"

"I don't know," conceded Rose.

"All I'm saying," said Effie, "is that I've been reading *The Illustrated Crime News* from cover to cover for weeks now, and one of the things I've learned is that when the police are investigating a murder, they don't begin by asking who killed the victim, but rather, why the victim was killed."

"That may be," said Rose impatiently, "but what we can be certain of is that, with a little nudge from us, Sir Godfrey is about to topple off his pedestal, and just in time to save Grace from marrying him."

There was the sound of a carriage outside. Effie looked out. The first guests were already arriving, and Sir Godfrey was among them. Aurora said that they must go down and greet them. As they reached the drawing room, Lucy the parlourmaid stopped and told them that Thomas, Grace, Edward and Freddie had arrived a few minutes earlier around the rear of the house and had gone up by the back stairs to get ready. Edward would lend Thomas some evening clothes and they would be down shortly. Edward had requested that the girls hold the fort for them and greet the guests.

"Is Freddie all right?" asked Rory.

Lucy nodded. "The walking wounded, but no serious harm done by the looks of it, miss."

Rose wondered about the nature of the accident that had befallen the boy. Could it have been bullying that caused his injuries? The doorbell rang loudly, announcing the arrival of the first guests.

"Smile," instructed Aurora, looking tense.

"Should I go upstairs and speak to Thomas about Sir Godfrey?" asked Rose.

"It's too late," said Aurora tersely. There was the sound of voices in the hall, and of coats and wraps being handed over.

"We'll just have to sit through the dinner and tell them about Sir Godfrey afterwards," said Rose.

"Might be tricky," said Aurora. "He's one of the guests staying the night. Along with his sisters, their husbands and a countess who Sir Godfrey insisted was invited too. We may just have to be patient and wait until the morning when everyone has left. It would be awful if there was a big scene."

The girls could hear the voices moving towards the drawing-room door, when there was a tap on the French windows that led down into the garden. Edward was standing there adjusting his tie. Rose ran and unlocked the door, and as Sir Godfrey and guests swept into the room, the four of them stood in a line to greet them, smiles fixed upon their faces.

"Have you got the emeralds?" whispered Aurora.

Edward nodded. "In my pocket. I made an excuse for stopping off at the bank on the way back. I shall return them first thing in the morning, and we can retrieve them for Grace to wear at the wedding, if that is what she wants to do."

"About the wedding…" said Aurora, but she got no further, as a beaming Sir Godfrey bore down upon them.

* ✳ *

Madame de Valentina was in full flow, delighting Sir Godfrey's sisters and the countess with her card tricks. They had moved upstairs to the Chinese drawing room, and Rose was sitting next to Thomas towards the back of the room. She had a good view of Grace, sitting to one side of de Valentina. She was next to Sir Godfrey, who held her hand firmly in his, as if worried she might run from the room. Grace looked tired and pale, and she kept glancing towards the door, as if she wanted to get away and be with Freddie. Edward and Rory were sitting next to them and both seemed preoccupied. While everyone was having drinks, Rose, Rory and Effie had taken the chance to creep upstairs and find Freddie. Perdita was sitting with him, tenderly stroking the child's face. The boy was fast asleep, but they could see the black eye and the broken arm.

"Bullying?" asked Rose softly.

Perdita nodded. "Grace believes so, although of course the school denies it. They say the child must learn to toughen up."

Rose made a face and whispered, "So what they are really saying is that Freddie should learn how to be a bully himself."

Perdita nodded. "I believe that sums the situation up. But at least Grace has decided that he should not return."

Good, thought Rose to herself. It was one more reason why Grace had no need to marry Sir Godfrey.

"You can start teaching Freddie again," whispered Rory. "He loved that."

"Maybe," said Perdita, a look of sadness in her eyes.

* ❌ *

Madame de Valentina continued her act, so familiar from Campion's, although with only the card trick and hypnotism components.

"She should stick to the hypnotism. She shouldn't do card tricks up close in full light where we can see every move," whispered Effie, who was sitting on the other side of Rose.

Rose nodded. Effie was much better at card tricks. It made Rose think about de Valentina's act. It may be popular with the Campion's crowd, but it was an ill-conceived mish-mash, as if it had been thrown together. Why didn't she just do the hypnotism? She was clearly good at that. After all, that was what Pony Snatchwitch told them she had originally been booked to do at the Alhambra. The communing with the dead element seemed to be another add-on, like the card magic. It had been undeniably popular and profitable, but even Madame de Valentina herself seemed to have lost interest in that section of the show, as if it had outlived its purpose.

"She's leaving. After tomorrow's show," whispered Thomas in Rose's ear. Rose looked up at Thomas with a frown as he continued. "Can't say I'm sorry, although we will take a financial hit. There is a touch of the night about her – she makes me think of a vampire, the way she appears and vanishes, always in her onstage costume, never joining in with the day-to-day of Campion's life."

"Where's she going?" hissed Rose.

Thomas shrugged. "She mentioned something about returning abroad. It's strange. She was so keen to come to Campion's, and she's only been here a few weeks. She could easily top the bill until Easter if she wanted. Clearly we've served our purpose, whatever that was."

Somebody in the row in front turned around with a frown. Elenora had moved on to the hypnotism segment of her act. Rose was bored of it by now. She had seen it enough. Aurora was being beckoned up on to the stage, and Rose felt sympathy as Rory rearranged her features from horror to acquiescence, as Sir Godfrey insisted she oblige Madame de Valentina. Edward's mouth was set in a grim line. He clearly wasn't thrilled at the prospect of his daughter being made a spectacle of, but there wasn't much he could do. Rose felt relief that she was hidden away at the back and hadn't been called up on to the makeshift stage.

She just hoped that de Valentina didn't make poor Aurora do anything too embarrassing. But, as if knowing that would be inappropriate in this particular company, Elenora was restrained. When she rang her little bell after whispering in Rory's ear, all that the glazed-eyed Aurora did was say the alphabet backwards, stand and sit, pretend to take a dog for a walk, and sing "Three Blind Mice" at de Valentina's command. It was all very polite, and quite as dull as the card tricks.

Rose was relieved when the gong sounded and they all trouped into dinner. Particularly when she overheard Effie in full flow telling the countess about her personal experience of slum life in Shoreditch, and what she'd like to do to absentee landlords who charged impossibly high rents to the poor for insanitary housing.

After they had eaten dessert, Edward briefly left the table and returned with a black velvet box. He quietened the chatter by tapping on his glass with a spoon.

"My dear Grace," he said. "These are a wedding gift to you from Rory and me." He opened the box and lifted the Easingford Emeralds up so that they caught the light.

"Oh, Edward – I cannot accept such a generous gift," protested Grace, but Edward held up a hand to silence her and fastened the necklace around her neck. The emeralds glinted, and Sir Godfrey's eyes glinted admiringly too. The table clapped, and Grace expressed her thanks.

"They are beautiful, Grace," said Aurora. "And so are you. The Easingford Emeralds couldn't have found a better home."

"By rights they should be yours, Aurora," said Grace gravely.

Rory shook her head vigorously. "I don't need to own them. I have more than enough."

Rose looked around the table – at the silverware, the gold-embossed crockery, and at the people sitting around it, in all their finery, with their pearl necklaces and gold rings, and thought that Rory was right. Everyone sitting around the table, herself included, had more than enough.

"A toast!" said Sir Godfrey.

He poured a little wine into one of his own unused glasses, handed it to Grace and raised his own glass.

"To my beautiful fiancée, Grace." He paused. "And to Edward and Aurora, for their generous gift." He clinked his glass with Grace's and said, "Drink, my darling! Drink to your benefactors."

* ✳ *

Rose woke with a jump and sat up in bed. She had been having a dream, and in the dream she could hear a bell ringing – a distant tinkle. But some other sound had woken her. It was very dark. Her eyes adjusted to the gloom. She, Aurora and Effie were all sharing a huge double bed in a large bedroom with heavy furniture inlaid with a dragon motif. The bedroom overlooked the square. She slipped out of bed and went to the window, pulling back the thick damask curtains so that she could look out. Silver Square was in darkness. She turned back to the bed. Effie was fast asleep, snuffling like a hedgehog with both arms flung up over her head. But Aurora was missing from the bed. The door to the room was ajar. Perhaps she had gone to get water? Rose realised how parched she was – all that rich food had given her a thirst. She padded towards the door, and as she reached it, Effie sat up and said sleepily,

"Where are you going, Rose? And where's Ror?"

Rose shrugged. "I don't know. I woke up and she was gone. I'm going to get some water. Maybe that's what she's doing too."

Effie scrambled out of bed just as the church clock struck three a.m. "I'll come with you. I don't want to be alone in here with them dragons giving me the evil eye. They're creepy."

Rose held out her hand. "Come on. I don't want to be wandering round a great house like this on my own."

"Me neither," said Effie. "I don't know how Ror can stick it here. Or those people. That sister of Sir Godfrey's is a real snob. The way she kept looking at me made me think she'd be advising Edward to count the spoons before I leave."

"Don't be daft, Effie. You've as much right to be here as anyone else. In fact, rather more right than Sir Godfrey's snobby sister."

The girls headed to the staircase. They were on the third floor of the house, in the bedroom next door to the one in which Freddie was sleeping. As they reached the final flight that led to the second floor, they caught a glimpse of a cotton nightdress, as somebody turned the corner at the other end of the corridor, as quietly as a ghost. The door to Grace's room stood wide open. It was strange – Rose had noticed when they had trouped up to bed that Grace had already retired for the night, and that her door was fast shut. Through the door, Grace could now just be glimpsed fast asleep in the bed, a single candle still burning by her side, as if she had fallen asleep before she could snuff it out. The door must have blown open, thought Rose, as she stepped forward to pull it back closed. As she did so, she saw movement in the room, beyond the bed. She gestured to Effie to join her and her eyes grew wide. Aurora, dressed only in her white nightdress, was standing by the dressing table in front of the looking glass. Her back was to the girls. But her image was reflected in the looking glass, and Rose could see that Rory was clasping the black velvet box containing the Easingford Emeralds in her hands. There was something about her reflected face and empty eyes that made Rose shiver.

"Aurora," she hissed, but Rory didn't hear. She was turning the case over and over in her hands, shaking it and muttering anxiously under her breath. Rose could only make out broken words.

"Emeralds … stairs … emeralds … window … drop … do as instructed … no good ... gone…"

"Rory!" said Effie louder.

Grace stirred and turned in her bed, and at that moment came a pitiful cry from above them. Freddie! Rose and Effie turned and ran up the stairs, and as they did, they heard another bedroom door open further along the corridor. Glancing back, Rose saw Sir Godfrey's door open. It stayed ajar, as if someone was behind it, listening. But she didn't hang around because Freddie cried out again.

It was at least twenty minutes before they had soothed Freddie, who had clearly had a bad nightmare. Eventually he sank back into a deep sleep, and the girls returned to their room. Aurora was lying in the bed, fast asleep. Rose frowned when she saw her.

"What do you think Rory was doing in Grace's room?" whispered Effie, seeing her sleeping like a baby.

"I don't know," said Rose. "She seemed anxious. Not like herself at all."

"Well, Edward did say last night how pleased he would be when the emeralds were safely back in the bank. Maybe the thought disturbed

Rory's dreams, and she went to check they were still there."

"Perhaps that's the explanation. But it's very odd," said Rose, going to the curtain and peering out. "We can ask her in the morning what on earth she thought she was doing. I wondered whether she might be sleepwalking. She looked so strange. Somebody else was up – a woman. I glimpsed her nightdress. And Sir Godfrey's door was open too."

She looked across the square. Two cloaked figures were hurrying across the road from the direction of the house. She couldn't see their faces, but she got a sense from their body language that they were arguing, and arguing furiously. There was something familiar about them. She turned back to the bed. Effie was already asleep. She was dead tired too. Rose looked at her two friends, both sleeping the sleep of the innocent, and she smiled. Then she clambered into bed and was asleep herself in seconds.

19

Rose opened her eyes and blinked. There was shouting on the floor below. She could hear Sir Godfrey's irate voice. Somebody was weeping loudly. She shook Rory and Effie awake, and they ran downstairs. Rose wondered whether somehow Sir Godfrey's hypocrisy and lies had come to light, without her and her friends revealing what they had learned about him two nights ago when they had gone to St Paul's Cathedral.

But it soon became clear that was not the reason for the uproar. Everyone was still in their nightclothes and dressing gowns. The countess was wrapped in a paisley shawl, wearing large slippers, a tiara perched on her head. Rose wondered whether she slept in it. Edward was running his hands through his hair, his face concerned.

"Are you quite certain that you left the necklace in its box on your dressing table, Grace?" he asked. "You couldn't have hidden it elsewhere and forgotten where you put it?"

"No, no, no," keened Grace, rocking back and forth. "I am so sorry, Edward. You entrusted me with a family heirloom, and it was just a few hours in my care and it's lost."

"Lost!" shouted Sir Godfrey's sister. "How can you mislay a valuable necklace in the middle of the night? No, it's not lost. A burglar got into the premises during the night and has stolen it."

"Grace, you mustn't blame yourself," said Edward. "It's not your fault. You didn't help yourself to your own emeralds."

"Yes, but somebody did," boomed the countess. "Thank goodness Inspector Cliff is on his way. He will discover the villain who committed this terrible crime."

Rose had to suppress a smile – given their past experiences with Inspector Cliff she didn't have the countess's faith in the Inspector's ability to solve crimes. She glanced uncomfortably at Effie, who she could see was anxious. Should they say that they had seen Aurora in Grace's bedroom holding the box containing the necklace? But Rory would never take the emeralds – not in a million years – and it felt disloyal to mention it, particularly as Rory had gone to sit by Grace, and was getting her to explain how she had discovered the necklace was missing.

Rose was quite relieved when the door opened and Inspector Cliff was shown in.

He nodded to everyone and got straight down to business.

"I understand there is no sign of a break-in?"

"That's correct," said Edward.

"An inside job! Just like at Lady Plockton's and the Fitzcillian residence," said the countess. "You can't trust servants these days," she sniffed. She turned to the Inspector. "You should search all their rooms immediately."

Edward bristled. "I have complete faith in everyone who works at Silver Square. Everyone who was here last night is still here this morning. I would trust them all with my silverware, and my life."

The countess snorted. "Then more fool you, Edward Easingford. Servants are always light-fingered when they get the chance. Dishonesty is bred into them. It runs through their bones."

"I don't believe that," said Edward, quietly but firmly.

The countess glowered.

"So," said one of Sir Godfrey's sisters, directing her gaze at Edward, "if you believe that the servants are quite innocent of the theft, are you suggesting that one of us took the necklace? Because if you are, I will not stay in this house a moment longer."

Edward sighed. "I am simply saying that I trust all of my employees."

The woman nodded at her husband. "Cyril, we are leaving…"

"Actually, madam," interjected the Inspector, "you will all have to stay a while yet as I conduct my initial inquiries. But I will be as quick as I can, and you will be able to leave very shortly, I'm certain. Please sit down."

Everyone, some with more reluctance than others, found a chair.

"Good," said the Inspector. "Now, explain to me what happened last night."

Edward spoke, telling of the performance, the dinner, the presentation of the necklace to Grace, how they had said goodnight to those guests who were not staying, and how everyone then retired to bed. Everyone nodded, corroborating what Edward said.

"Did everyone know where the emeralds would be overnight?" asked the Inspector.

Thomas spoke. "Yes, because I suggested to Edward that perhaps it would be safer if he kept the necklace in his room, rather than leaving it with Grace, and we were all present when he asked her if she would like him to take responsibility for it. But she said she was sure it would be perfectly safe in her room."

"Mr Campion, did you have any reason to be concerned for the safety of the necklace?"

"No," said Thomas. "But like everyone else, I did know that it was valuable."

The Inspector turned to Grace. "Where did you put the emeralds?"

"On my dressing table. I didn't take them out of the box."

"Did you leave the room at all after placing them there?"

Grace shook her head. "I went straight to bed. I was exhausted. I could barely keep my eyes open long enough to get into bed."

The Inspector looked around the room. "I want

you all to answer the next question individually. Did any of you leave your bedrooms at all during the night?"

The Inspector asked each of the women in turn: Grace, Perdita, Sir Godfrey's sisters and the countess. They all denied having left their beds. Rose frowned. Somebody was lying. Unless she had seen a ghost, one of them had been out of bed during the night – she had seen a nightgown. Why would they lie?

The Inspector turned to the men. Again, they all denied having left their bedrooms. Cliff looked at Aurora.

"Did you leave the bedroom you were sharing with your friends?"

"No," said Rory serenely. "I was in the bed all night."

Rose and Effie looked at each other aghast, and tried to hide their discomfort, though not very successfully. The Inspector swung around and gazed hard at Rose.

"And you, Miss Campion – did you get up and leave your room in the night?"

"Yes, Effie and I got up to go in search of a glass of water," said Rose uncertainly.

"Did you find one?"

Rose shook her head. "No, we were going downstairs when we heard Freddie cry out, and we rushed back up to his bedside."

Effie nodded in agreement.

"And while you were out of bed, did you notice anything unusual?"

Rose flung Effie a desperate glance and then looked beseechingly at Aurora, who was looking at her with a sweetly puzzled expression. Rose couldn't bear to meet her eyes.

"Yes," she whispered. "I did. I saw... I saw..." Her voice had become inaudible. Everyone was staring at her.

"What did you see?" asked the Inspector gently.

"I saw Rory in Grace's room. She was holding the box containing the emeralds. She was shaking it and then she opened it and peered inside, and she seemed distressed."

Aurora gave a wounded cry and her eyes were incredulous. "But that's not true, Rose! I never left my bed. You're my friend! Why would you lie like that?"

"She's not lying," said Effie, who had begun to cry. "I saw you too, Ror."

"She did," said Rose, wringing her hands.

"But there must be an explanation…" She tailed off lamely.

Aurora looked wildly around the room, and then, with her chin defiant but her eyes full of hurt and tears, she said, "Does anyone else want to accuse me of stealing the emeralds?"

Sir Godfrey cleared his throat. Rose realised he had been uncharacteristically quiet up until now.

"I saw Miss Easingford too, with the emeralds in her hand."

The Inspector looked at him like an inquisitive cat. "I thought you said you didn't leave your room?"

"I didn't. But I did peep outside my door, and I saw Miss Easingford walking down the stairs. She was holding the emeralds."

"What time was this?"

"Just after three a.m. I glanced at my pocketwatch."

Aurora shook her head and looked at him, her eyes full of contempt.

"Maybe you'd like to explain, Sir Godfrey, what you were doing out of bed?" asked Rory. "Perhaps you had an assignation? Perhaps you had some urgent business at St Paul's?"

There was a tiny frozen silence, and a small earthquake seemed to take place on Sir Godfrey's face, as shock and horror did battle with outrage.

Rory continued. "Perhaps you'd like to explain about the earrings you sent to Ivy, and the single earring that you sent to Jenny, who plays Prince Charming, after the first night of the pantomime, inviting her to meet you at St Paul's at midnight, where you would be waiting."

"This is preposterous! The girl is a liar as well as a thief," thundered Sir Godfrey, though he had visibly flinched at the name Jenny and had turned quite pale.

"She isn't lying," said Rose quietly. "Effie and I saw you at St Paul's too. I've got the proof as well – the note and earring are both in my possession. Would you like to see them, Inspector? It might be crucial evidence in your ongoing investigation into the murder of Ivy Puddlewick."

The Inspector nodded.

"Look here now, what are you insinuating?" demanded Sir Godfrey, and there was a mixture of bluster and fear in his voice. "The note you have might have been sent by anyone, and I certainly have never had any assignations at St Paul's. I have never been so insulted in my life. I am a man of integrity. These music-hall guttersnipes are all lying, and trying to point a finger at me in order to draw attention away from the fact that Aurora Easingford is a common little thief who stole her own aunt's wedding gift."

There were a number of "hear hears" from Sir Godfrey's sisters and their husbands.

"Sir Godfrey," said Edward warningly, "that is my daughter you are calling a common little thief, and my closest friends you are calling music-hall guttersnipes, and you are doing it under my roof."

Grace stepped forward. "And Aurora is my niece, and Rose and Effie are both my friends, and I know them all to be as honest as the day is long. Which is more than I can say for you, Sir Godfrey. What kind of engaged man sends notes and earrings to another woman?"

She loosened the engagement ring on her finger and held it out to him. "Our engagement is terminated."

He snatched it from her, and said, "I wouldn't marry into this family if you paid me."

Rose had to suppress the urge to pipe up, "But that's exactly what Edward did," but she managed to hold back the remark, knowing that this would hurt Grace.

Sir Godfrey turned to the Inspector. "Am I free to go, or do you plan to arrest me?"

Inspector Cliff took his time before he answered. Rose thought he had the look of a man who was enjoying himself.

"For the time being, yes, you can leave. But I will certainly have further questions for you about your relationship with Ivy Puddlewick, and the woman called Jenny."

He turned to Thomas. "If I understand correctly, this Jenny plays Prince Charming in the pantomime – is that right?" Thomas nodded. "And where might I find her?"

There was another tiny silence, and then, with a big grin, Grace spoke up.

"Here. I play Prince Charming under the assumed name of Jenny Roberts."

There were loud gasps from the countess and Sir Godfrey's sisters.

Sir Godfrey looked like a tree that had just had an axe taken to its trunk. But then he collected himself, brought his scowling face close to Grace, and hissed in the meanest of voices, "I always knew you were no lady. But I was prepared to overlook it and take you and your brat on, out of the goodness of my heart and misguided generosity. You and the rest of the Easingfords will regret trying to make a fool of me."

He stalked from the room, followed by the rest of his party, who bustled after him like flapping chickens, pecking at the words "scandalous", "disgusting" and "outrageous" as they went. Rose heard one of the sisters asking Sir Godfrey where he was going.

"To St Olave's. I need some quiet, reflective time alone."

20

For a few minutes everyone sat in shell-shocked silence. The Inspector asked some further questions about the missing emeralds and then left to talk to his men, who were busy quizzing the servants and searching the square. He came back several moments later with a black velvet box, which he asked Edward and Grace to identify as the case that had contained the emeralds. They did.

"One of my men found it tossed in the bushes in the square. Quite empty of course," he said, before returning to his men.

There was another long silence, then Grace said in a small voice, "I know there are more pressing matters, but I suppose we will have to make an announcement about the cancellation of the wedding."

"Leave it to me, Grace," said Edward. "I will deal with it."

Rose wanted to fling her arms around Aurora, but her friend was sitting so stiffly, with her mouth in such a grim line, that she hardly dare look at her, let alone touch her.

"Rory," she said hesitantly. Aurora almost flinched at the sound. "Rory, I'm sorry. I don't for a second think you stole the emeralds, but Effie and I can't deny what we both saw, any more than you can deny that you saw Sir Godfrey outside St Paul's Cathedral."

"I understand," she said quietly. Her face crumbled. "But I'm so frightened. You say I was in Grace's room and I had the box with the emeralds in my hands, but I have absolutely no recollection of it. It makes me think that I must be losing my mind."

Edward gathered her in his arms and hugged her hard.

"Maybe you were sleepwalking," said Perdita thoughtfully.

"That must be it," said Edward eagerly. "Rory, we'll send for Dr Neagle. He will be able to advise us."

"But what if Inspector Cliff arrests me for stealing the necklace?" wailed Rory.

"I don't think the Inspector will be in any hurry to arrest you," said Effie firmly. "Not after the mistake he made in arresting me for a murder I didn't commit. He still looks guilty every time he sees me. He's not going to make that mistake twice."

"Besides," said Edward, "he can't arrest you if no crime has been committed."

"What do you mean?" asked Grace.

"Well, I will simply tell the Inspector that we were mistaken, and that the necklace was not stolen but misplaced, and that we would like to withdraw our complaint because there was no robbery. There would be nothing he could do."

For a moment Rory looked relieved, but then she frowned and said, "But that wouldn't be true. The emeralds *have* been stolen. If you do what you suggest, while nobody will ever openly dispute it, for the rest of my life people who know what happened – and I'm certain Sir Godfrey and his sisters will deliver a highly edited and damning version of what occurred here this morning to all their friends – will look at me and wonder if I really did steal them. Maybe all of *you* will sometimes look at me sideways and think, 'Maybe she did take them'. So thank you, Edward, but no thank you. I would prefer to wait to be proved innocent, however painful the process."

"That's very brave of you, Rory," said Thomas.

Rose thought so too, particularly as there was no certainty that the Inspector would ever solve the mystery. The Plockton and Fitzcillian robberies were still unsolved. She frowned.

"There is one thing that definitely doesn't fit the scenario of you stealing the emeralds, and the Inspector must realise it. This robbery bears an uncanny resemblance to the Fitzcillian and Plockton robberies. There must be a connection between the three thefts, and the connection clearly isn't you."

"Well," said Aurora doubtfully, "we do know both families, and I've been to their houses."

"Maybe you have, but you weren't present in their homes when the robberies took place. There must be something else that connects the thefts. Whatever it is, I'm certain it's not you. If only we could work out what it is."

Everyone started discussing excitedly what they thought it might be, and Rose took a moment to speak to Grace.

"Are you all right, Grace?"

"Never better. I am so relieved to be rid of Sir Godfrey. I've had a lucky escape." She paused and looked at Rose. "Do you think he could be Ivy's killer?"

"I don't know," said Rose. "He is undoubtedly a hypocrite and a liar, but that doesn't mean he's a murderer too."

There was a knock at the door, and Lucy entered with a silver tray piled high with white envelopes. She looked on the verge of tears and couldn't meet Edward's eye.

"These have come," she said in a whisper.

Edward looked puzzled as he took the top envelope and opened it. He glanced at the contents and tossed it away with a curl of the lip. He opened the next and crumpled the contents up. He picked up a third and opened it.

"What is it, dear boy?" asked Thomas, seeing his face. Edward raised the embossed letter and with a raised eyebrow read out loud. "Lord and Lady Fortune regret that they will not be at home this Thursday or at any Thursday in the future." He pointed at the other envelopes, "They are all in a similar vein. Every drawing room in

London is closing its doors to us. Clearly Sir Godfrey and his sisters are very quick workers. The Easingfords are outcasts in London society."

"Oh, Edward, I'm so sorry," said Grace.

Edward laughed. "I'm not."

"Me neither," said Aurora.

"The only thing I'm sorry about is that I let myself be ensnared by high society for so long." Edward picked up the remaining envelopes and tossed them into the fire without reading them.

"This is over. Let's gather our belongings and go back home to Campion's as soon as we can. I'll tell the Inspector where he can find us."

Rose gave a little smile at his use of the word "home". She caught Rory's eye, who smiled back.

"Of course," said Thomas. "I must get back anyway and cancel the pantomime for tonight."

"Cancel the pantomime?" asked Edward.

"Well," said Thomas. "I thought that nobody would feel like doing it after everything that's happened."

"I've never been more up for doing it," said Edward. "But I think it's up to Rory and Grace. They may feel very differently. It's their decision."

Grace looked at Aurora. "I'd like to do it, but it's your choice, Rory. Everyone will understand if you feel you can't."

"But I can do it," said Rory. "It will take my mind off what has happened. There's nothing like being on stage for forgetting your worries. But I will only do it on one very important condition."

"What?" asked Grace.

"I'm going to perform using my own name, Rory Easingford."

"And I will play Prince Charming under my own name too," said Grace. "No more pretending to be what I'm not."

21

In the end it was already late afternoon and the sky was darkening by the time that Rose, Effie and Aurora made their way back to Campion's alone. They had spent part of the morning playing with Freddie, who, despite his injuries, was in high spirits now that the threat of having to return to school had been lifted. Perdita had come to find them, and Rose was struck by how gentle and loving she was with him. On occasion, Rose looked up and found Perdita staring at her with a strange expression on her face, as if she was about to say something to her.

Grace and Perdita were still busy packing, and Grace also wanted to spend some time alone with Freddie, so the girls had set off to Campion's alone. Thomas had already left, as he had other business to attend to in the city.

After he had drafted a statement announcing that the wedding had been cancelled, Edward had set about organising the closing-up of the house. It would take until well into the new year, and he was determined not to do it until everyone who worked there had secured a new position.

All day there had been a steady stream of cards and letters from members of the aristocracy, making it quite clear that Edward, Aurora and Grace would no longer be welcome in their homes. Rose wondered if Sir Godfrey would receive the same treatment if his behaviour ever became public.

Rose and the others walked across London Bridge as new flurries of snow began to fall. They cut down the side of the river, past the mudlarks, who called out to them.

"We saw that big cat last night. It's almost fully grown."

Rose nodded, but she was worried – not just for the tiger itself, but also for the citizens of Southwark and Bermondsey. It may have been playful as a cub, but a fully grown tiger stalking the streets could pose a significant danger, particularly if its food sources dried up.

They arrived back just in time to see Madame de Valentina disappear through the stage door, ready for the early show.

"She's leaving after tonight's show," whispered Rose to the others.

Both of them were surprised.

"But why, when she's indisputably top of the bill?" asked Rory.

"That's what Thomas asked when he told me," said Rose. "He said we must have served our purpose."

"But she was so keen to come here," said Effie. "Even before poor Ivy was killed."

"I know, it's so odd," said Rose. "She—" Suddenly she stood still and touched her forehead. "Of course! That's it! A motive for Ivy's murder."

"What do you mean?"

"Well, we already know that when Hopkin and Dent were booked to replace Ivy, they were threatened to the point that they were sufficiently frightened into deliberately performing so badly that Thomas asked them to leave. That left a vacancy – one that Elenora filled. Maybe Ivy was murdered because she was too good.

Nothing except death was going to knock her off the top of the bill at Campion's!"

"So are you saying that you don't think Sir Godfrey had anything to do with Ivy's death, but perhaps Madame de Valentina did?" asked Effie with a frown.

"Or maybe the two of them were working together," said Rose thoughtfully.

"But why – and to do what?" asked Rory. "Thomas must be paying Madame de Valentina handsomely, but surely not enough to make it worth killing Ivy."

"Rory's right," said Effie. "It doesn't add up. You need to slow down, Rosie. You practically accused Elenora of killing Pru's mum, so maybe you should speak to the Inspector and hold back before you start going around saying you think it's probable she's a murderess."

Rose nodded, but then she said excitedly, "But maybe I was right about her killing Pru's mum. If she would kill to make sure she got top spot at Campion's, wouldn't she also be prepared to kill to make sure she stayed there? Appearing to commune with the recently deceased would be a sure-fire way of doing it."

"Maybe," said Effie. "But she would have

had to have accomplices to make that happen, because she couldn't be in two places – Campion's stage and Pru's home on Lant Street – at the same time."

"That's true," said Rose. "But don't you remember, Effie, that when we went to Lant Street to collect Pru's suit from Mrs Smith in the afternoon, she apologised for not having it ready and said she was delayed because a woman she didn't know had knocked on the door claiming to have lived there previously, and she had shown her around? She even made her tea. Maybe that woman was trying to get a sense of the layout of the place. Perhaps Mrs Smith even showed her the hiding place where the St Christopher was found."

"And," said Effie excitedly, "Pru mentioned answering the door to another woman when she came home. Perhaps it was a deliberate distraction, so that the murderer could get in through the back door, kill Mrs Smith and put the St Christopher in the hiding place."

"Whoa," said Aurora. "Until we've got a good reason for why Elenora was so keen to stay top of the bill, it's all just speculation, Rosie. You don't have any real evidence that she has committed any crime at all."

"Rory's right," said Effie. "You can't go round making accusations until you're sure. Believe me, I know what it feels like to be accused of something I'm sure I didn't do."

"Me too," sighed Rory.

An hour later, Rose and Rory were helping Ella in the kitchen, while Effie helped backstage, setting up the props for the evening show. They were telling Ella what had happened at Silver Square. Rose thought how easy Ella was to talk to, and she idly wondered about trying out her theory about Madame de Valentina on her. She had noticed Ella's antipathy towards de Valentina, so maybe she would be more receptive than Effie and Rory. But Ella was very interested in what had occurred at Silver Square, and had stopped washing dishes and was listening to Aurora carefully.

"Oh, you poor child," she said, as Rory explained her hurt and confusion when Rose and Effie spoke about seeing her at Grace's dressing table, holding the box containing the emerald necklace. "How deeply distressing. You must have been distraught to have your friends so insistent about what they saw."

Rose suddenly thought of Florrie, who had been similarly accused by her friends of being out of her bed on the night of the Plockton robbery.

Ella frowned and asked if anything unusual had occurred early in the evening.

"No," said Rose. "It was an immensely dull evening. I'd have much rather have spent it here at Campion's. The food was lovely, particularly the chocolate cake, but Sir Godfrey and his sisters were terrible snobs. I hate to say it, Rory, but even when Madame de Valentina hypnotised you so you said the alphabet backwards it wasn't very interesting."

"Elenora hypnotised Aurora?" asked Ella sharply. The girls nodded. Ella sat down on the kitchen stool as if her legs had buckled. "Well, that explains it," she said, but she almost seemed to be speaking to herself. "I knew there had to be a bigger reason for why they did what they did." She had turned very pale, making the pink scar on her forehead even more visible.

"Ella!" said Rose. "What do you mean?"

"I'm not entirely sure yet," she said slowly. "You may be able to help me. But if there is one thing of which I'm quite certain, it is that Rory is telling the truth when she claims to have no memory of leaving her bed, and that you and Effie are also telling the truth about what you saw. Rory doesn't recall being in Grace's room holding the box with the emeralds, because she wasn't really herself. She was acting under the influence of hypnosis."

The girls gasped.

"Is that possible?" asked Rose. "I know Madame de Valentina can make people bark like dogs, but can she make them steal emeralds? Because if she can it would explain why she was so keen to come to Campion's, and why she wanted to ensure that she stayed here."

Ella nodded. "I've been asking myself the same question," she said. "Do you trust me, Aurora?" asked Ella. Rory nodded. "Then I will demonstrate. In fact, it might throw some light on exactly what happened. Rose, go and get me Madame de Valentina's silver bell. I imagine it will be on the props table, ready for her performance."

Rose ran to the table, picked up the bell and then called down the trap for Effie, who emerged, covered with grease, as Rose beckoned her to follow her back to the kitchen. She wasn't sure exactly what it was that Ella was going to demonstrate, but she felt a frisson of excitement about it and wanted Effie to be there.

Back in the kitchen, Ella locked the back door and the door leading into the auditorium.

"Are you ready, Aurora?" she asked.

Aurora nodded. Ella rang the bell, and as its tinkle sounded, a frozen look crossed Aurora's features. It was uncannily similar to the look that Rose had witnessed on Florrie's face in the kitchen, that day when the sound of Madame de Valentina's bell had penetrated the kitchen from the auditorium.

"Aurora," said Ella gently. "Can you hear me?" Aurora nodded. "Aurora, I want you to show me what happened in Grace's bedroom last night."

Rory glided forward like a ghost, her eyes unseeing.

"You are in front of Grace's dressing table," intoned Ella. "What are you looking for?"

"The emerald necklace," said Rory, and her hands started moving over an invisible surface, as if looking for something.

"Why do you want the emeralds?" asked Ella.

"I've been told to get them," said Aurora.

"Who told you to get them?" asked Ella.

Aurora frowned and became distressed. "I am not allowed to say," she whispered, and then she started reciting the alphabet backwards. Rose and Effie looked at each other. Madame de Valentina had made Rory do that when she hypnotised her.

"Can you see the black velvet box on the dressing table?" asked Ella.

"Yes," whispered Aurora, her eyes still spookily unseeing.

"What are you going to do with it?"

"Pick it up," whispered Aurora.

"And then what will you do with it?"

"I will check the necklace is inside, and then I will take it downstairs to the kitchen, where I will open the small window by the back door and drop the box out of it."

"Show me what you did last night," said Ella.

Aurora's hands floated in front of her, and suddenly it was as if she had picked a box up. She shook it and then she frowned, and then made to open the invisible box and stared down into it. She was whispering to herself frantically.

"No necklace. Where emeralds?" As her distress increased, her language broke down.

"Emeralds … stairs … emeralds … window … drop … no good … gone…"

"Show me what happened next," commanded Ella.

Aurora turned around and appeared to be walking down imaginary stairs, and then she walked again and seemed to be miming opening a window and dropping something outside.

"What are you dropping Aurora?" asked Ella.

Aurora frowned. "Box. No emeralds."

"Aurora," said Ella very quietly, "are you telling me that the velvet box you threw out the kitchen window was empty?"

Aurora nodded. "No emeralds in the box. I looked. But not there. Angry voices outside window." She began to cry. Ella rang the little bell, and immediately Rory stopped crying, put her hand to her wet cheek, as if surprised to find it damp, and said, "So when are we going to start the demonstration?" She looked dazed.

Ella took her hand and said very kindly, "The demonstration is over, Rory."

Aurora laughed. "But I haven't done anything yet."

Ella smiled softly. "You've shown us

everything we need to know."

"But I don't remember anything," said Aurora, looking scared.

"No, you won't," said Ella. "You were acting out what you did at Silver Square, after Madame de Valentina implanted instructions in your mind when she hypnotised you. You were to go to Grace's room, find the box containing the emeralds, take it downstairs and drop it through a pre-planned window, where the thief would be waiting to catch it. She implanted the idea in your head in the Chinese drawing room after she hypnotised you. When she whispered in your ear, she wasn't just whispering that you were to recite the alphabet backwards, but also telling you that later that night you were to steal the emeralds and drop them out of a designated window. The signal that you were to act upon that order would have been the ringing of a bell, just like this one. It may be small, but the sound is unexpectedly penetrating, and even the most distant tinkle would make the hypnotised victim – in this case you – comply with the instructions Elenora had sown in your head to steal the emeralds."

"She must have done the same thing to

Florrie, who worked at Lady Plockton's," said Rose excitedly. "And, Rory, I remember you saying that some of the Fitzcillian servants had been hypnotised too – and then that house was robbed shortly afterwards."

"And it would explain why she wanted to come to Campion's, because of the number of toffs and their servants who come here."

"Yes, it would explain why she would go to any lengths to be top of the bill," said Ella grimly.

"And why she told Thomas that she would be leaving. She knew that she was about to get the greatest prize of all: the Easingford Emeralds," said Rose.

"Except that she hasn't got them," said Effie. "Ella's demonstration proves that Aurora didn't steal the necklace. Under hypnosis, she did indeed go to get it, but the box she dropped out of the window was empty."

Rose thought about the two figures she had seen hurrying across Silver Square, and the empty box found tossed in the bushes. Had they flung it away in their disappointment?

"You mustn't get your hopes up," said Ella. "If it came to it, and Aurora was arrested and stood trial, what I've demonstrated probably wouldn't be admissible in a court of law."

"Maybe not," said Rose thoughtfully. "But there is something else it shows. If Aurora never actually had the emeralds in her hands, it must also mean that Sir Godfrey was lying when he said he saw her with them on the stairs."

"It does," agreed Effie. "And it also means that the emeralds had already gone missing before Aurora tried to take them."

"So who has got them?" asked Rose.

"If, as we believe," said Ella, "Madame de Valentina was behind the attempted theft by Aurora, then I imagine that is also a question that she, and her associates, will be asking. I don't want to worry you, but it could make her very dangerous indeed."

"What do you mean?" asked Effie.

"Well," said Ella. "She won't know that the box was empty when Rory found it on Grace's dressing-room table. She might think that something went wrong with the hypnosis and that Aurora simply pocketed the necklace herself. And if she does, she will stop at nothing to get it." Ella touched the scar on her head. "I know just how ruthless she can be."

"I'm going back to Silver Square to get the

Inspector," said Rose. "Elenora is due on stage very soon. When she comes off, I'm going to make sure that she is greeted by the police."

22

Rose set off at a run. Her head was swirling with thoughts, and she realised that in all the excitement, she had entirely forgotten to ask Ella how she knew how to hypnotise people. She was beginning to suspect that if Madame de Valentina was not all that she seemed, then perhaps Ella wasn't either. She realised that she didn't even know her second name.

Perdita was walking purposefully towards her up Hangman's Alley. Her eyes softened when she saw Rose.

"Is Ella in the kitchen?" she asked. Rose nodded. "Good. I need to talk to her. Rose," she said hesitantly. "I've got something that I want—"

"Sorry, Perdita, it'll have to wait. I'm off to find

the Inspector. There have been developments."

She reached the end of Hangman's Alley and was rounding the corner, wondering whether she should also send a message to Scotland Yard in case the Inspector had gone back there, when she ran slap bang into Florrie and Col.

"I can't stop," said Rose.

"But I've got something for you," said Florrie, putting her hand on her arm. "I know you will want to see it." She thrust a piece of paper into Rose's hand. "I found this among my uncle's belongings. I told my aunt that you had asked about *The Winter's Tale* at the Imperial Grand, and she said he kept the programme of every production staged while he worked there. She remembered the story of the baby going missing. Apparently, the baby was the daughter of the lead actress playing Hermione, and she was left in the care of another actress, the one playing Perdita. My aunt can't recall all the details, but apparently there was some question of negligence on the part of the actress playing Perdita. Something about jealousy too."

For a moment, Rose starred at Florrie, and she felt as if the world had tipped on its axis. She was about to discover the name of her mother.

She looked down at the programme, hardly able to see the words written there, her eyes so blurred with tears.

Her eyes focused and she saw the name of the actress playing Perdita: Portia White. She scanned the paper again. The name of the actress who had played Hermione danced in front of her eyes: Elenora Valentine.

For a moment she thought that she might faint. The world seemed to be spinning and she could barely breathe. But then the confusion that fogged her mind cleared, and she felt in her pocket for some money, handed it to Florrie and said urgently, "This is important. We need to get Inspector Cliff to come to Campion's as soon as possible. Florrie, you must get a cab to Scotland Yard in case he is there, and, Col, you must go to thirty-two Silver Square. He may still be there. He must come at once. Tell him it's about the Easingford Emeralds, and that I sent you."

"Are you all right, Rose?" asked Florrie. "I would never have shown you the programme if I thought it would upset you so."

"I'm fine," said Rose. "But please go now. We must get the Inspector to Campion's. It's urgent."

Seeing her grim face and haunted eyes, Col asked curiously, "What are you going to do, Rose?"

Rose gave a hollow little laugh. "I'm going to say hello to the long-lost mother I've been looking for all my life."

* ✻ *

Rose slipped back inside Campion's via the stage door. O'Leary was asleep on a chair. She walked down the corridor almost blindly. She felt bereft. All her life, she had been hoping against hope that she would find her mother. Secretly she had longed for her to be an actress – preferably one who had acted the great classical roles. Now she had found her, and discovered that she had indeed once been an actress, but Rose also knew that she was almost certainly a thief, and maybe a murderess too. She felt a tangled mixture of sadness and anger. All she knew was that, before the Inspector arrived and almost certainly arrested Elenora, she wanted to have one chance to talk to her mother alone, and find out about the circumstances of her birth. At the door of Madame de Valentina's dressing room she hesitated. She could hear raised voices within.

"You double-crossed me and you'll pay for it," said a gruff voice that sounded vaguely familiar, but which Rose couldn't place.

"I did no such thing. You have double-crossed me. Or else we have both been fooled," came a second voice in reply.

"What do you mean?" asked the first voice.

"The only explanation I can think of is that the hypnosis was not quite strong enough, and the girl did as instructed and took the emeralds, but then woke up for some reason and decided to keep them for herself."

"Why should I believe you? Maybe when the girl was at her most suggestive you implanted another idea in her mind, and she dropped the necklace somewhere else before tossing the empty box through the window where we were waiting. Maybe you went back later to get the emeralds, to keep them for yourself."

"And risk making a permanent enemy of you, and a bullet in the back? I would not be so foolish. We have both been robbed, and I suggest we stop the recriminations, cut our losses and get as far away from here as fast as we can."

"After all this planning I'm not going to let the greatest prize slip through my fingers. We must go after the girl and get her to hand over the necklace."

"You can do what you want. Tonight is my last performance and then I will be gone. My half of the proceeds from the Plockton and Fitzcillian robberies will have to suffice. If you want to pursue the emeralds, that is your business, and if you recover them from the girl, you are welcome to the proceeds. But I will leave on the train for Calais tonight."

"Don't be so certain."

"Are you threatening me...?" asked the first voice, but got no further, because at that moment Rose flung the door open. She expected to find two people inside. But only Madame de Valentina was there, quite alone. Rose looked wildly around, but there was nobody. Then she spotted the dressing-room window that looked out over Hangman's Alley. It was wide open – the conversation she had heard must have been conducted through the window. The other party had clearly scarpered at the sound of Rose's entrance.

"Have you been eavesdropping?" asked Elenora de Valentina, grabbing Rose by the arm, her eyes steely and narrowed. Rose shook her head and Elenora let go of her arm. "Then what do you want?"

Rose hesitated for a moment, and then she whispered, "I just wanted to say hello to my mother."

Elenora frowned and made a shrugging gesture with her hands, and with mock exaggeration started peering around the dressing room.

"Your mother? I don't think I see her here."

Tears sprang into Rose's eyes. "You," she whispered. "You are my mother. Elenora Valentine. The Elenora Valentine who played Hermione in *The Winter's Tale* at the Imperial Grand, and whose baby was stolen from a pram outside the theatre."

A look of complete incredulity crossed Elenora's face, followed by one in which the truth dawned on her.

"You think that I am Nell Valentine?"

"Yes," whispered Rose.

Elenora began to laugh – a harsh, unpleasant sound.

"Oh, Rose, you silly goose," she said. "I'm not your mother."

"Yes, you are," said Rose fiercely. "You lied to me and told me that my mother was dead because you didn't want me to find out the truth." Then, angrily, she continued, "We've worked it out. You killed poor Ivy Puddlewick so that you could get top billing at Campion's, and hypnotised people so that they would unknowingly rob and steal on your behalf. You're a charlatan and a liar and a murderess. The police are on their way."

Elenora had stopped laughing and was staring at Rose. She started stuffing things into a bag.

"Yes," she said coldly. "I am a charlatan and a liar. But I am not lying when I say that I am definitely not your mother, Rose. I was telling the truth that night in Lant Street when I said that your mother is dead. She is. I'm sorry, Rose, but I saw it happen with my own eyes."

"You're lying," shouted Rose, all the hurt of the last thirteen years rising in her chest. "Why don't you want to admit that you are my mother, and acknowledge me as your daughter?"

"You are mistaken, Rose. I am not your mother. It is impossible," said Elenora, and her tone was softer. She took a step towards Rose, as if to take her hand.

But as she did so, a shot rang out from the window. Madame de Valentina crumpled forward into Rose's arms and they both collapsed on the floor. As she fell, Elenora's wig fell off and Rose found herself staring down into the face of a man – a man whose features were familiar from the police "Wanted" posters that had been plastered all over the newspapers. The person pretending to be Elenora de Valentina was Ambrose Skelly, better known as the Cobra. He gave a wry smile.

"So you see, Rose Campion. I was not lying when I said that I could not be your mother. I simply took your mother's identity after she was murdered."

"She is really dead?" asked Rose, her voice quavering.

Ambrose nodded.

"If you didn't kill her, who did?" asked Rose.

"The same person who has just done for me," said Ambrose. "The Duchess. She hit poor Nell Valentine over the head and threw her into the Thames. The poor woman didn't stand a chance."

Volcanic rage rose through the whole of Rose's body, making her shake.

"Where will I find the Duchess?" she whispered.

"If she is still around here, she's most likely to be found in the graveyard. We were using one of the mausoleums as a safe place to leave messages," replied Ambrose. "But take care. She is armed and dangerous. Get the police to go with you, Rose. Don't go alone."

Rose suddenly recalled the exchange she had heard between Ambrose and the Duchess.

"Is Aurora in danger?"

"I fear so," said Ambrose. "I'm afraid I led the Duchess to believe that Aurora Easingford took the necklace. She will resort to anything to get it."

"But Aurora didn't steal the necklace, did she," said Rose slowly.

"No," said Ambrose serenely, though he was clearly having trouble breathing. "The Duchess was right. I did double-cross her. I intended to do so right from the start. I came to an agreement with Godfrey Caskins. He has long been a useful contact for me – feeding me interesting information about people in the higher echelons of society. It was he who told me that the Easingford Emeralds would be here in London. He was furious that Edward Easingford was giving the emeralds to his fiancée, Grace, and that they would be her personal property. Godfrey would be quite unable to touch them. The man has urgent money problems. It was why he wanted to marry Grace Easingford, in the hope of getting his hands on some of the Easingford fortune. He is a deeply unpleasant man. I did try to warn Grace on my first night at Campion's, by pretending that I had made contact with her late husband, Ned. No women should be expected to put up with such a man. He is a swindler and a fraud and he has catastrophic debts. He has been helping himself to the money from the charities he runs for years, and it's all about to come tumbling down. He'll be exposed unless he gets his hands on substantial amounts of money very quickly."

Ambrose continued between laboured breaths.

"I used the emeralds as a way to get the Duchess to help me – it was her idea that I use my hypnotism skills to get others to steal on our behalf. It couldn't have worked out better when it turned out that Nell Valentine was coming to London. We simply intercepted her at Euston Station, dumped her in the river and I assumed her identity.

"But then Thomas Campion refused to book me, because of that two-bit Ivy Puddlewick at the top of bill. So we had to take further action. Then, to ensure I stayed top of the bill, the Duchess came up with the idea that if people could be persuaded that I could talk to the dead, my position at Campion's would be unassailable. It was brilliant but time consuming – all that hanging around graveyards. But her real coup was coming up with the idea of me communicating on stage with Prudence Smith's mother before anyone knew she was dead."

"How did you manage it?" asked Rose, aghast at his matter-of-factness.

"It was simple, really," said Ambrose. "The Duchess knocked at the door earlier in the day and found out as much as she could about the place from Mrs Smith. Then, later, the Duchess and Godfrey Caskins kept watch until Prudence returned. Then the Duchess knocked again and kept Prudence distracted while Godfrey slipped in the back door, used chloroform on Mrs Smith and pressed her face into the cushion. Then he took off the St Christopher around her neck and put it in the hiding place that Mrs Smith had told the Duchess about in the afternoon. He is a man of many talents, is Sir Godfrey."

"He murdered Pru's mum," whispered Rose.

"I'm afraid so," said Ambrose. "But if it's any small comfort, he was going to get his comeuppance tonight. We had an arrangement to meet in the graveyard after I had completed my final performance. He was going to hand over the necklace, and I was going to give him the money I had agreed with him: my share of the Plockton and Fitzcillian robberies. Of course, I had no intention of doing so. Once he had handed over the necklace, I would have slit his throat and left him for dead." He gave a little humourless laugh. "Look how our fortunes have been reversed."

"You don't deserve one, but I'll get you a doctor," said Rose, scrambling to her feet.

"Too late for that, I think," said Ambrose. Rose was already at the door when he spoke again.

"You know, from the moment I arrived at Campion's, I always thought that you were the person who was most likely to see through me. It's why I pretended to be speaking to your dead mother that night in Lant Street. I wanted to crush you. But you are un-crushable. If I had ever had a daughter, Rose, I would like her to have been like you."

23

Rose ran along the corridor calling for help, and people came running, spurred by the urgency in her voice.

"Luke," she gabbled, "run for Dr Neagle. Madame de Valentina has been shot and needs help, only she's not who she says she is. She is actually Ambrose Skelly. Hurry."

She sent Lottie to find a policeman – as many as she could. She hoped that by now Inspector Cliff would be on his way to Campion's. She wanted to go to the graveyard to try and find the Duchess, but she knew that Ambrose was right. She must wait for the police, but with every second that passed she felt as if her heart would burst with the tension of waiting. She went to return to Ambrose's side, but at that moment

Effie appeared, running across the stage.

"Rose," said Effie. "It's Rory. She's disappeared."

"Missing?"

"Yes," said Effie. "Rory got a message from O'Leary at the stage door, asking her to meet Edward in St Olave's graveyard. Said it was urgent. But then Edward arrived and I told him where she had gone, and he said it must be some mistake because he had sent no note. After what Ella said, about whoever did steal the emeralds thinking that Rory had pocketed them, I thought I better go to the graveyard and see."

"You're right," said Rose. "We've got to go, and now. I know who sent that message."

"Who?" asked Effie.

"The Duchess. She wrote it to lure Rory to St Olave's. She believes that Aurora stole the necklace. There isn't a moment to lose."

They set off, shouting at O'Leary to inform the others where they had gone, and to redirect Inspector Cliff to the graveyard as soon as he arrived.

As they ran, Rose gave Effie a potted version of what Ambrose had told her. Effie's eyes grew round, particularly at the revelations of

Godfrey's involvement. As they approached the graveyard, Effie said, "We should split up. Do you know which mausoleum the Duchess hides out in?"

"Not for certain, but I think it could be the one we hid in on the night the Tanner Street boys tried to kill the tiger. Somebody had clearly been there recently."

Effie nodded. "You approach from one side and I'll take the other."

Rose nodded grimly.

The only thing they had on their side was surprise. If the Duchess was indeed holding Aurora, their only chance of overpowering her would be if they startled her. At least they would be three against one. They crept through the graveyard, past the ravaged stone angels with disfigured faces, and around each side of the mausoleum as quietly as possible. At the entrance they paused, holding their breath. They could hear no sound from within. Rose stepped forward into the darkness, fearing that she would find Rory's lifeless body inside.

Then a voice from behind them said, "Stay where you are, and put your hands up if you want Aurora Easingford to live."

It was the Duchess. She had them trapped. Rose felt like a fool. After everything she had heard from Ambrose, she had felt the need to pursue Aurora to the graveyard immediately. The Duchess might well kill all three of them and get clean away, unless they could keep her talking until help arrived. The girls raised their hands slowly and turned around. The Duchess had tied Aurora's hands together behind her back and she was pointing a pistol at Rory's temple.

"One false move and I pull the trigger."

Rose wasn't going to argue. Aurora's eyes were liquid with fear. The Duchess tickled Rory's temple with her pistol.

"I'm going to ask one last time, and if you do not tell me the truth I'm going to blow your brains out. Where have you hidden the emeralds?"

There was a tiny pause, and Rose sensed movement in a distant part of the graveyard. She shifted her head very slightly. She could see a figure moving in the shadows, clambering over the graves. She couldn't be sure, but she thought it was most likely Sir Godfrey. The Duchess's view was obscured by the mausoleum behind her. Rose suddenly had a rush of certainty. It was

Sir Godfrey, and she knew why he was there: he had come to retrieve the necklace, as agreed with Ambrose. And she was certain she knew where he had hidden it: in the gap at the base of Effie's mother's headstone. It was a perfect hiding place. She might be signing their death sentences by doing so, but she had to speak out.

"Aurora didn't take the necklace, but I know who did."

The Duchess narrowed her eyes. "Enlighten me, Rose Campion. Or should I say, Rose Valentine. Who stole the emeralds?"

Rose felt the ripple of shock pass through Rory and Effie's bodies at this news. She had told Effie what had occurred in Madame de Valentina's dressing room, but she had not mentioned that she had originally gone to confront her because she had mistakenly believed that Elenora was her long-lost mother.

"Godfrey Caskins stole them. He was in league with Ambrose. You were right, Duchess. They double-crossed you. They were going to cut you out of the deal and share the proceeds themselves."

"Why should I believe you?"

Rose took a deep breath and said, "Because if

you look to your left now, you will see Godfrey attempting to retrieve them from their hiding place under the headstone of Effie's mother's grave."

For a second the Duchess hesitated, but then she turned her head, and as she did so Rose kicked out at her, grateful for all those years spent learning the cancan. The gun skittered out of the Duchess's hand.

"Run!" she called to Effie and Rory. "Get help."

Rose reached down for the gun but the Duchess was on her, and although she was older than Rose and far less agile, she was heavier and she pinned Rose to the ground. Rose saw Effie and Rory hesitate, and Rose shouted, "Get help" again, and there was something so terrible and commanding in her tone that they obeyed her.

The Duchess and Rose rolled across the ground, and the Duchess's hand found the gun first. She grabbed at it, raised it and fired it. Rose winced at the whipcrack sound, but then she realised that the Duchess was not pointing the gun at her, but at Sir Godfrey. She had grazed his arm. The Duchess was up and after Sir Godfrey, who was crouching by Effie's mother's tombstone, frantically scrabbling in the earth. The Duchess was firing wildly, fury and greed affecting her aim. Rose ran after her and ducked just in time, as Sir Godfrey returned fire. The Duchess tripped over a tree root and fell, her gun cartwheeling into the bushes. But, seeing Rose pelting headlong towards him, Sir Godfrey raised his gun once again and took direct aim at Rose. He went to squeeze the trigger, but as he did, a shot whizzed towards him from the other side of the graveyard, hitting him expertly in the thumb and knocking the gun out of his hand. It bounced across the ground and out of reach. The bullet had taken his thumb clean off. Blood poured from his hand and he was bent double in pain.

"Stay exactly where you are," commanded a voice, "or it will be my great pleasure to take off your other thumb too." It was Perdita, remarkably calm and collected and standing atop a small hillock. "There's no point looking for the emeralds, Godfrey. I've already taken them from their hiding place. I guessed it was you who stole them. I saw you slip a sleeping draught in Grace's drink when you insisted on that toast at the end of the evening, and I assumed you must have had a very good reason for doing so."

The Duchess was rising painfully to her feet, her back to another of the broken-down mausoleums that dotted the graveyard.

"Stay right where you are too, Duchess," said Perdita. "Rose, pick up both of their guns and give them to me."

Rose walked gingerly forward towards the bushes, but as she passed by the Duchess, the woman lunged at her with the speed of a snake trapping its prey. She caught Rose and held a second gun to her head, backing them both into the entrance of the mausoleum. The Duchess gave a devious smile.

"You underestimated me, didn't you, Perdita Black? Did you really think I would have only one weapon? Shoot me and this meddling child will die. Or maybe I should address you as Portia White, as I believe you were once known."

Rose suddenly recalled the programme for *The Winter's Tale*. The actress playing Perdita, the one who Florrie said was supposed to be looking after Rose when she had been stolen from her pram, had been called Portia White. She frowned. Could Perdita, the woman standing here before her, be the same woman whose negligence had led to her loss?

Perdita saw her confused face. Without lowering the gun, she said, "I'm afraid the Duchess is right, Rose. I am indeed responsible for your disappearance from the pram outside the Imperial Grand. I was supposed to be looking after you. Your mother had paid me handsomely to do so. But just as she was leaving, she told me that she was going to see the manager at another theatre, about playing Viola in *Twelfth Night*. She just happened to mention that he had told her that none of the other actresses he had seen were up to the role, and it was hers for the asking. What she didn't know was that I was one of those actresses. In fact, I was confident that the role was already mine, although nothing had been agreed. I was already jealous of Nell Valentine's abilities. I was even jealous of her baby. To hear that I wasn't good enough fuelled my jealousy and resentment.

"She went off. A few minutes later, you woke up. You were crying and I couldn't settle you, so I put you in your pram outside the theatre where I couldn't hear the noise. Of course, I regretted it almost immediately, but when I returned just a few minutes later you were already gone, stolen away. Two days later the police found a baby's body in the river. Nell was in no state to identify the body. It was her second loss in just a few months – her husband had died of consumption just weeks before you were born – so I identified the body. It was such a tiny little thing, so small and defenceless. I thought it was Nell's child." She began to weep.

"Later when I went to look after Freddie, of course I heard your story, and how you had been left on the steps at Campion's. But I never made the connection between you and Nell Valentine's child. Why would I? I believed that I had identified your tiny drowned body. It wasn't until the day Inspector Cliff turned up, saying he had discovered you had been snatched from outside the Imperial Grand, that I made the connection and started to wonder if I had made a mistake when I identified that poor babe. I'm not asking you to believe me – but barely a waking moment passes when I don't regret what I did. Even my dreams are haunted by it. When I lost that poor baby, I lost myself too. I changed my name to Perdita Black to remind me of my negligence every day, and I resolved never to step foot on stage again."

"What a nice little sob story," said the Duchess.

"I don't expect any sympathy," said Perdita quietly. "I fell as low as it was possible to fall. I was living on the streets. I applied to one of Sir Godfrey's charities for help, and I was refused. But then I saw a notice pinned inside the porch of St Olave's, with a list of all the women and children and families who had been given help by his charity. My name was there. I started asking around, and discovered that the names of the poor who had been refused aid regularly appeared on the lists of those who had received it. So where was the money going? Was he lining his own pockets? I started to help in a school, and gradually I got my life together, and eventually started to work as governess. When I was employed by the Easingfords and came across Sir Godfrey again I decided to keep a close eye on him, and find out what I could, because I was convinced he was a cheat."

"You are a liar," said Sir Godfrey. "Who will ever believe anything you say – a woman known for her negligence and the loss of a child."

He started to try to crawl away on his knees, and Perdita fired a warning shot. Rose could see someone making their way across the darkness of the graveyard, nimbly darting between the gravestones. She decided to try and keep everyone talking.

"I can see why you wouldn't make the connection between me and the lost baby," said Rose. "But when you came to Campion's, weren't you concerned that Elenora de Valentina and Nell Valentine might be the same person, and your past would come back to haunt you?"

"As soon as I saw her on stage I knew it wasn't the same person," said Perdita. "It was clear that the name was merely a coincidence. In any case, the Nell I knew was an actress, not a hypnotist."

"Ah," said another voice. "I learned those skills to survive in America." Ella suddenly stepped out from behind a gravestone very close to Perdita.

"You! Nell Valentine!" said the Duchess, and she turned white. "You are dead! I hit you over the head and dumped you in the river."

"You did," said Ella, "but Nell Valentine is a survivor." She smiled at Rose. "And now I want to talk to my daughter. My Rosalind, as I called her. My Rose by any other name."

Her eyes were full of tears as she held out her hand to Rose and took a step forward. As she did so, the Duchess fired directly at her. Perdita flung herself in front of Ella, taking a bullet to the arm and dropping her pistol. The Duchess would have fired again, but Inspector Cliff's voice carried across the graveyard.

"You are surrounded, Duchess. You cannot get away."

"Then what do three more deaths matter?" she said, with her gun trained on Rose's head. "Shoot me, and they die too."

Rose could see the Duchess's finger on the trigger. Her eyes were granite. She had no doubt that the Duchess would do exactly as she said. She closed her eyes and just hoped that Inspector Cliff didn't bungle this one. This wasn't the kind of scenario that she had imagined when she had daydreamed about being reunited with her long-lost mother.

"I want safe passage," said the Duchess.

"No chance," said the Inspector.

"Refuse me and I will kill them one by one."

"I will not negotiate," said the Inspector.

But Rose wished that he would – at least long

enough to keep her alive. The Inspector may have the graveyard surrounded, but no one could take out the Duchess from behind, with her back protected by the large stone mausoleum. She started to drag Rose back into its mouth.

"I'm going to count to three, and then it will be the final curtain for Rose Campion," said the Duchess, and she sounded as if she was enjoying herself.

"One... two ..."

There was a sudden roar from behind the Duchess, a flash of fur and stripes, and the tiger rushed from out of the mausoleum and was on the Duchess. With a scream, the Duchess fell sideways, dropping the gun and releasing Rose from her grip, who managed to stumble forwards into Ella's arms. Despite her wound, Perdita darted forward and retrieved the fallen gun. But there was no need. The tiger had pinned the Duchess to the ground and was snarling in her face.

The Inspector's policemen appeared from all sides of the graveyard, followed by Thomas, Effie, Rory, Edward and Grace, and surrounded the Duchess and the tiger. Some of the policeman eyed the tiger nervously. Several had their guns raised.

"Don't shoot," cried Rose.

Hearing her voice, the tiger looked up, jumped off the Duchess and sauntered to where Rose and Ella were locked in an embrace. The tiger purred and weaved between their legs, rubbing its head against Rose's knees, purring loudly.

The Duchess, snarling as loudly as any tiger, and Sir Godfrey – his head bowed in shame – were taken away by the police. Thomas hurried towards Rose and Ella. Ella looked up at him and smiled.

"My name is Nell Valentine. You have done a wonderful job bringing up my daughter, Thomas Campion. I couldn't have wished for her to have a better father."

She held out her arm to encompass him in their embrace and Rose thought that this was what it really felt like to have a family of her own.

24

Rose and the rest of the *Cinderella* cast stood in a blizzard of snowflakes on the Campion's stage, taking their final bow. It was Christmas Eve. Rose glanced along the line at their shining faces. One face shone more brightly than anyone else's: Ella's. Or rather, Nell Valentine's. She was as luminous as one of the stars in the night sky. Everyone was still getting used to calling her by her real name. Nell, as she was now known, had just played Cinderella for the first – but not the last – time.

Dolores had given up the role with alacrity, saying that acting really wasn't her thing, and that as Nell was a "proper" actress she would do a much better job. She had, and the Campion's audience had immediately taken Nell to their hearts, as if she had been performing on the Campion's stage for her entire life. Rose looked up the line again and Nell beamed at her. There was such love in the smile, and so much happiness that Rose thought her heart might burst. She still couldn't get used to the word "mama" on her tongue.

"I don't know how I ever thought I could live without this," breathed Grace, who was standing to one side of Rose. The crowd stamped their feet and called out Grace's and Rory's names. Grace was going to continue to play Prince Charming for the rest of the pantomime run. Pru had said that she had quite enough on her plate now she was back at the top of the bill, and besides, she preferred singing to acting.

The audience was calling for Thomas to come on stage, and he clambered up with a big grin on his face as he caught Ella's and Rose's hands and gave a bow. Rose thought she had never felt happier. Everything she longed for had come true.

They came off stage, where Perdita was waiting for them. Her meagre luggage was stacked up beside her. She was clapping as best she could with her wounded arm done up in a sling.

"I just wanted to say goodbye to you all. I must go soon if I'm to get the boat train to Liverpool." She was going to America to put the past behind her and begin again. Edward had paid for her passage.

Perdita pulled Nell towards her and hugged her.

"I did you a great wrong, Nell. My jealousy caused the loss of your baby. I thought that I could never forgive myself, but your forgiveness has meant everything to me. Thank you. I will never forget your generosity."

"Are you sure you won't stay, Perdita?" asked Rose. "At least spend Christmas with us all. You would be so welcome."

Perdita shook her head. "I would love to, but I won't. The longer I stay, the harder it will be to leave. And I must be brave and begin again." She smiled pensively. "Perhaps in America I might even start acting again."

Tomorrow Campion's would be closed. Great trestle tables would be set up on the stage, two huge turkeys would be roasted in the kitchen ovens and all of the Campion's staff who were without relatives – a great many of them –

would join in the feasting. Pru would be there, and Lottie and Jem and O'Leary, as well as some of the servants from Silver Square, and all the mudlark families. But that was tomorrow. Tonight, there was still one more thing to be done.

* ✳ *

Rose and the others paid off the cab and hurried towards the dark entrance to the Zoological Gardens in Regent's Park. Edward was carrying a sleepy Freddie in his arms. Mr Burns, the Zoological Gardens director, was waiting for them, wrapped in a heavy cloak with a scarlet muffler. He shook hands with everyone and then he took a large key from out of his pocket and unlocked the gate.

"Of course, this is strictly against the rules," he smiled, with a twinkle in his eye. "And if anyone ever asks, it never happened. But when I heard what had occurred, and what a good friend you have been to the tiger, Rose, I wanted to give you all a small Christmas present."

They followed him along the zoo's winding paths, past the sleeping giraffes and the monkeys. But they didn't stop until they reached their destination – the big-cat enclosure.

Rose ran forward to the side of the cage, and the tiger, which had been dozing in the corner, looked up, stretched and then padded over to Rose and put its muzzle between the bars. Rose scratched its nose, and the tiger purred. "You saved my life," she whispered. "Thank you."

Mr Burns beckoned Rose round to the front of the cage.

"As you are theatre people, I thought we should have a little theatrical flourish at our ceremony," he said with a smile, pointing to a pair of small red velvet curtains attached to the wide wooden panel that ran around the cage beneath the protective bars. "Rose, would you like to do the honours?"

Rose bent and pulled the curtains back. Underneath was a small brass plaque engraved with the legend: "Ivy Puddlewick. Siberian tiger." Everyone clapped.

"The tiger's female then?" asked Rose.

Mr Burns nodded.

"Oh, Ivy would have loved this," said Rose. "Having a tiger named after you is even better than being top of the bill at Campion's."

"We are already confident that the animal will be one of the zoo's star attractions. She's drawing the crowds," said Mr Burns.

After saying their goodbyes to Mr Burns and the tiger, the party arrived back at Campion's just as flakes of snow began to fall. It was an unusually clear night. The moon was bright – a silver disc hanging amid the winking, blinking stars. Somewhere in the distance they could hear someone singing "Silent Night", and they all joined in, their voices rising and falling in the icy air. They reached the front door of Campion's, and Rose went to pass by it and enter through the stage door as they always did, but Thomas stopped her, and pulled out the key to the great front door, which was decorated with painted garlands of fruit and over which was written the legend: "Campion's Palace of Varieties and Wonders".

"Rose," said Thomas. "These are the very steps where I first discovered you as a baby. Maybe I am being sentimental, but I would like the joy of watching mother and daughter walk up them and over the threshold into Campion's together."

Thomas unlocked the heavy door. Rose and Nell gazed at each other for a moment, and then they smiled, linked arms and walked up the steps. Rose felt as if she was walking into her future.

Rory and Effie rushed up the stairs and threw their arms around the pair, as Grace, Edward, Thomas and Freddie looked on, beaming. Rose put out her hand to them and pulled them into the circle. Everyone she loved was here, and Campion's had never felt more like home.